Sawyer winced sli~~g~~ some antiseptic o~~n his arm.~~

"All right, I patched you up as well as my medical expertise will take us. But I take no responsibility for anything if you get gangrene and your arm falls off." Megan began to put away the first aid kit then stopped and just threw it on the counter. "This place is going to have to be burned to the ground anyway."

She turned away and looked back into the bedroom. Sawyer put his shirt back on.

"You can't stay here. Even after the police process it, it's not safe for you to stay here."

"I know." Megan's words were soft, her look lost.

Sawyer reached down and grabbed her hand, entwining their fingers together. "We'll make it through this together. But right now we need to get out of here in case our vicious friend decides to come back with friends of his own."

COUNTERMEASURES

Janie Crouch

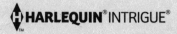

HARLEQUIN® INTRIGUE®

To my dear, sweet Megan. I count it as one of
life's greatest blessings that you and I found
each other again. You are a treasure. I promise
to never leave you in another vat of ice for as
long as I live. Here's to our adventures of the
past, the present and the future.

ISBN-13: 978-0-373-69817-2

Countermeasures

Copyright © 2015 by Janie Crouch

Recycling programs
for this product may
not exist in your area.

Printed in U.S.A.

www.Harlequin.com

Janie Crouch has loved to read romance her whole life. She cut her teeth on Harlequin Romances as a preteen, then moved on to a passion for romantic suspense as an adult. Janie lives with her husband and four children in Virginia, where she teaches communication courses at a local college. Janie enjoys traveling, long-distance running, movie-watching, knitting and adventure/obstacle racing. You can find out more about her at janiecrouch.com.

Books by Janie Crouch

Harlequin Intrigue

Omega Sector series

Infiltration

Countermeasures

Primal Instinct

Visit the Author Profile page at Harlequin.com for more titles.

CAST OF CHARACTERS

Sawyer Branson—An agent for Omega Sector, an interagency task force made up of the most elite agents the country has to offer. He's being sent to babysit Dr. Fuller as reprimand for insubordination, and he's not happy about it.

Dr. Megan Fuller—Beautiful computer scientist who discovered a problem with the Ghost Shell technology she helped design a year ago. Now someone will go to any lengths to make sure she's not able to develop the countermeasure for Ghost Shell.

Fred McNeil—Former FBI agent and current head of crime syndicate group DS-13. He tricked Megan into giving him Ghost Shell and plans to sell it on the black market.

Evan Karcz—Sawyer's best friend and fellow Omega agent.

Juliet Branson—Sawyer's sister and former Omega agent until tragedy struck.

Jonathan Bushman—Megan's assistant at Cyberdyne. A critical part of the development of Ghost Shell and the countermeasure.

Trish Wilborne—Peppy computer programmer at Cyberdyne. Does her smile hide suspicious activity?

Ted Cory—Head of security at Cyberdyne. Willing to do anything to keep Cyberdyne safe, including attacking first and asking questions later.

Dennis Burgamy—Sawyer's boss at Omega Sector. Seems to care more about his own reputation than the safety of his agents.

Chapter One

"Dude, I'm just saying, if you didn't want a terrible job assignment then you probably shouldn't have punched out your boss."

Sawyer Branson rolled his eyes and kept walking down the hall of the nondescript building that housed the offices of Omega Sector Headquarters. "C'mon, Evan," Sawyer told his fellow Omega agent. "I didn't punch him out. I tripped."

"Yeah, you *tripped* and your fist *accidentally* fell into Burgamy's jaw." Evan couldn't even say it without chuckling.

Hell, just about everyone at Omega couldn't say it without a chuckle now.

Sawyer stopped by his desk and began looking for a tie in the drawers. Okay, yeah, he had punched his boss two weeks ago, but only because it had been an emergency and his brother Cameron had been about to do much worse, like pull his gun on their boss.

So Sawyer had *tripped* and *accidentally* popped Dennis Burgamy—his supervisor here at Omega—right in the chin. But seriously, was it Sawyer's fault Burgamy had crumpled to the ground like a rag doll at the slightest tap?

Most importantly, though, due to the "accident" with Burgamy's chin, he and Cameron had saved Cameron's fiancée's life, arrested some very bad guys and pretty much saved the world.

Which had gotten Sawyer a two-week suspension without pay, thank you very much.

Sawyer rooted around in the drawer some more. Where was that damn tie? It was Sawyer's first day back and he wasn't about to walk into Burgamy's office without a tie, despite the fact that proper office dress was not high on the priority list at Omega Sector.

As a multiagency task force, Omega Sector had much more perilous concerns than whether or not the people who worked there—all handpicked and highly qualified—were dressed too casually. Sawyer, a five-year Omega veteran at thirty years old, especially did not worry about it. Usually.

Sawyer cursed under his breath as he continued his search for a tie, smashing a finger in one drawer while opening another. He heard a throat clear from behind his back and turned to find Evan swinging a tie from his finger.

"Thanks, man." Sawyer took the tie, figuring one with little golfers on it was better than no tie at all. "I'm just trying to do anything I can to get back toward Burgamy's good graces."

Evan gave a bark of laughter. "And also attempting to keep yourself from desk duty for the foreseeable future. Or the next twenty years if Burgamy has his way."

Sawyer rubbed a hand over his eyes at the thought of desk duty. The normal charm and charisma Sawyer counted on seemed to escape him—he had no idea what he was going to say to Burgamy in their meeting. Lord, Sawyer hoped it wouldn't come down to him being forced to a desk.

He was an agent. That was all Sawyer knew how to do. All he *wanted* to do.

And damn it, he was a *good* agent. Sawyer knew his strengths: he was likable and friendly. And people—witnesses, victims, hell, even perps a lot of times—had a way of opening up to Sawyer. Unlike his brothers, who tended to be the strong, sullen type, Sawyer was the strong, charming type. And people loved him for it.

He'd used his friendliness and charm to his advantage multiple times over the years. Sawyer just hoped he could figure out how to use them now when it mattered the most.

He gave another pull on the tie, straightening it at his collar. "Do I look okay?"

Evan gave the knot a mock straightening. "Yes, dear, you look as pretty as a princess."

Any other time Sawyer would've harassed Evan back, but he was too caught up in the thought of dreaded desk duty to bother. "Wish me luck, man."

Sawyer struggled not to compare the walk to Burgamy's office to a death march, but he had to admit he was distinctly nervous knocking on his boss's door. Not a feeling Sawyer was used to.

And damn his brother for all his falling-in-love stuff that had put Sawyer in this position in the first place. Sawyer would take his confirmed-bachelor existence any day.

Cameron entered the office at Burgamy's barked command.

Burgamy sat back in his office chair, dressed in impeccable officewear. His tie definitely had not come from a desk drawer, nor did it have little golfers on it. Burgamy obviously put a great deal of stock into the saying "Dress for the job you want, not the job you have."

Evidently the job Dennis Burgamy wanted was the director of the United States intelligence and/or fashion community.

Burgamy was always prepared in case he had to take an unexpected meeting with someone important. And often, Sawyer and his three siblings thought, went out of his way to make those meetings occur. Burgamy had butted heads with each of the Branson siblings, all of whom worked or had worked at Omega at one time or another. None of the Bransons liked Burgamy much. Although Sawyer was, to his knowledge, the only one of his family to have ever knocked his boss unconscious.

"Branson, come in and sit down," Burgamy told Sawyer without any pleasantries. Burgamy's nasally tone negated whatever credibility the man built with his impressive fashion sense.

Sawyer entered the room and sat at one of the chairs across from the desk.

"I want you to know that if it was up to me, you'd be fired right now," Burgamy began. Sawyer nodded; he didn't doubt it. "But since I'm the bigger man, and because your brother Cameron swears you actually tripped, I am willing to not push for your termination."

Sawyer didn't relax. Burgamy still had the authority to take Sawyer off active duty.

"Not to mention we have bigger problems than your lack of coordination or outright insubordination, or whatever you want to call it," Burgamy continued.

Sawyer nodded. "It won't happen again, sir. I can assure you of that."

Burgamy's eyes narrowed. "It best not, Branson. That little stunt you and your brother pulled? Well, you're damn lucky it all worked out the way it did or being fired right now—which you both would've been, believe me—would be the *least* of your problems."

Burgamy continued without even giving Sawyer the chance to speak. "The Ghost Shell technology in the wrong hands would be a disaster. Thousands of lives could be lost if terrorists got their hands on it."

Sawyer decided he better stick up for himself before Burgamy spun into a complete tizzy. "Absolutely, sir. But there was never any danger of the Ghost Shell technology falling back into DS-13's hands."

Sawyer didn't mention what an utter lie that was. Telling Burgamy that he and Cameron had basically delivered the encoding technology to the crime-syndicate group definitely wouldn't help Sawyer's case for non-desk-duty.

"Ghost Shell is in our custody, sir." Cameron continued with his most engaging smile. "So, all's well that ends well, as they say. And I really am sorry about the—" Sawyer made a popping sound with his tongue as he mimicked a punch to the chin.

Burgamy's eyes narrowed. "Well, Branson, I found out yesterday that all isn't as well as we think. You and your brother arrested Smith and some of the other key members of DS-13, but it looks like some others within the organization have taken Smith's place."

Sawyer wasn't surprised. In a crime organization the size and caliber of DS-13, removing one head usually just caused another, uglier one, to grow in its place. DS-13 was more than any one person; eliminating a single person— no matter how high up—would not bring the organization down.

"And we've found out that Fred McNeil, the FBI agent on DS-13's payroll, has gone completely off the grid," Burgamy continued.

"That's not surprising. McNeil had to know we'd be coming for him next. He's probably with DS-13 full-time now."

Burgamy nodded. "Intel confirms that he is. That's not the problem. Ghost Shell is the problem. We were able to trace Ghost Shell back to the company that made it." Burgamy slid a file across his desk to Sawyer. On the outside it was marked *Cyberdyne Technologies*.

Sawyer shook his head. "Cyberdyne. Can't say I've really heard of them."

"No reason you would have. They're a tech-development company based in North Carolina. Evidently, earlier this year one of their senior computer scientists got concerned about some software they were developing."

"Ghost Shell?"

"Yes. They were actually working on encoding technology for medical records and account-security type stuff. Then they realized Ghost Shell was something that could be used as a weapon if tweaked."

Sawyer nodded. He wasn't sure exactly how Ghost Shell worked, but he knew the results if it was used by a terrorist group: shutting down communication and computer systems within law enforcement and first-responder groups. Basically it turned the computers against themselves. If Ghost Shell was used in conjunction with a terrorist attack, the results would be devastating. Thousands of lives would be lost.

"One of Cyberdyne's computer scientists got concerned that something weird was going on at Cyberdyne. So, this—" Burgamy referred down to his notes. "Dr. Fuller contacted the FBI. Unfortunately the person put on the case was Fred McNeil."

"And Fred McNeil took the information given by said scientist and sent Ghost Shell straight to DS-13."

"Pretty much. Dr. Fuller had no idea Fred McNeil worked for DS-13. Of course, nobody did. Just bad luck all the way around."

Sawyer grimaced. The only bad luck was that Fred McNeil was still out there. Sawyer would like to take that treasonous bastard down. "But at least Cameron got Ghost Shell out of DS-13's hands before they could sell it to anyone."

Burgamy shook his head. "That's what we all thought. But we found out yesterday through a call to Cyberdyne that *two* versions of Ghost Shell were given to Fred McNeil."

Sawyer sat up straighter in his chair, his attention focused on Burgamy's words. "But we only recovered one."

"Exactly."

Sawyer clenched his jaw. "And McNeil still has it?"

"We've had no intel of him trying to sell it. Evidently even other members of DS-13 didn't know there was a second Ghost Shell. This second version wasn't entirely complete. McNeil needs somebody who can finish it for him."

Sawyer's thoughts spun. A not-working Ghost Shell was definitely better than the fully functional version; it gave them a little bit of time. But Omega Sector needed to begin active measures right away to keep Ghost Shell from becoming sellable by DS-13. An undercover operation would be the best solution, but difficult at this late a time. It had taken Sawyer's brother Cameron nearly a year of undercover work to truly infiltrate DS-13.

Omega didn't have that kind of time now.

"Okay, what's the plan?" Sawyer asked Burgamy. "I can try to set something up, call in a few favors to see if I can get in deep undercover with DS-13 quick. It's risky, but—"

"No, you won't be going undercover, Branson."

"Sir, I really think a quick, deep undercover mission is critical if we want to get Ghost Shell back."

"I agree that we're going to need to send someone in. But that someone will be Evan Karcz."

Sawyer knew his best friend, Evan, was highly qualified and even had an established cover that could probably work well in this situation. But Sawyer did not want to be left out of the action.

"I'll go in with him. He can use his buyer cover and I'll—"

"No."

Sawyer began to argue his case but then saw Burgamy's raised eyebrow and the way his boss sat back in his oversize office chair. The man wasn't interested in anything Sawyer had to say. Whatever was about to come next was Burgamy's retribution for Sawyer punching him two weeks ago.

Damn. Sawyer just hoped it wasn't a desk job at an outpost in Alaska.

"You will be heading to Swanannoa, North Carolina, for protective duty of Dr. Zane Fuller, the head of Research & Development at Cyberdyne Technologies."

Babysitting. Almost as bad as a desk job in Alaska.

Sawyer knew he had to make some sort of case against this assignment. "Sir, respectfully, I feel as if my talents may be better used somewhere else. Somewhere a little more…active." There was no way Sawyer wanted to spend the next couple of months babysitting some geriatric computer scientist. Not when there was real work that needed to be done.

"What's happening at Cyberdyne is active, Branson. Dr. Fuller at one time was working on a Ghost Shell countermeasure—a decryption system. That system being finished will be key if DS-13 finishes and attempts to sell the new Ghost Shell."

Sawyer grimaced. "I understand that and agree, but I just think someone else might be better suited for this particular job—"

"Someone who, say, isn't coming off unpaid leave for striking his superior officer?" There was the raised eyebrow again.

Sawyer shook his head and slumped back in his chair. All right, so Burgamy wasn't going to cut him any slack. Looking at his boss, Sawyer realized he wasn't getting out of this.

"All right, Cyberdyne it is." Sawyer spoke through his teeth with forced restraint.

"You'll be bringing Ghost Shell with you. Dr. Fuller needs it in order to complete the countermeasure system. Downright adamant about that. You'll have to explain what Fred McNeil did, and convince Dr. Fuller and the Cyberdyne team to help us." Burgamy didn't even try to hide the delight on his face. The thought of Sawyer having to deal with a grumpy computer scientist for the next couple of months in the middle of Nowhere, North Carolina, made Burgamy practically gleeful.

Burgamy had chosen Sawyer's punishment well; he knew how much Sawyer would hate this.

Burgamy filled Sawyer in on a few more details—none of which made Sawyer any more excited about the operation ahead. But fine, Sawyer would pay his dues, protect some old head of computer-nerdom for a couple of months, then get back to Omega, where he could do some real good.

And he would damn well make sure he never punched his boss again.

Chapter Two

Sawyer's arrival at the Cyberdyne Group Headquarters in Swanannoa, NC—more like Swananowhere, NC—the next afternoon did nothing to help reassure him that he would be doing any good in the fight against DS-13 while here. Sure, he could recognize the beauty of the Blue Ridge Mountains all around him. But he'd give it all up to be inside some sleazy warehouse somewhere, with no views but concrete and sewage, about to arrest some bad guys.

This place—no matter how beautiful the surrounding scenery—was a waste of his time.

Not that Cyberdyne and the work being done here was a waste of time, but as far as Sawyer could tell, Dr. Fuller and his cohorts were not in any danger. No attempts had been made on their lives, nothing out of the ordinary had been reported recently. Which was great. But it also meant that somebody with a little less experience in the field could be here completing this assignment rather than Sawyer.

Sawyer sighed and got out of his car. There was no point bemoaning this any longer. He cursed his brother Cameron once again on his way up the steps. This assignment from hell was all Cameron's fault for falling in love and trying to rescue the girl and save the world.

Sawyer rolled his eyes. Evidently Sawyer was a sucker

for a good love story. And this was what he got for it: Swananowhere.

Sawyer looked at the file again as he walked through the door. Cyberdyne Group had been around since 1983, a midsize company, mostly focused on conceptual and computer engineering. They'd done some contractual work for the US government over the years, but not as much as bigger corporations. Most companies similar to Cyberdyne in this area were located a couple of hours away in the Raleigh-Durham Research Triangle. But the original owner of Cyberdyne had loved the Blue Ridge Mountains so much he had built the Cyberdyne offices and labs just outside Asheville rather than Raleigh.

There wasn't a lot of information on Dr. Zane M. Fuller, the head of Research & Development at Cyberdyne—the person who had helped develop Ghost Shell and then turned it over to the FBI. Sawyer glanced at the file. Looked as if Dr. Fuller held *two* doctoral degrees from MIT—barrels of fun.

What the file didn't hold was any useful information about Dr. Fuller to help Sawyer plan out his protection detail. Was he married? Did he work fourteen hours a day? Did he have any bad habits that might get him into trouble?

Sawyer pictured a balding, cranky older guy with thick glasses and probably a bow tie. If that really was the case, Sawyer was going to take a selfie with Dr. Fuller and send it to Burgamy. His boss would probably cry tears of delight.

Sawyer might cry tears also, but they definitely wouldn't be of delight.

Sawyer made his way inside Cyberdyne, taking a few minutes to chat with the attractive and attentive receptionist at the front desk. Far be it for Sawyer to miss an opportunity to talk to a pretty lady, especially in a situation like this.

The receptionist called a security guard—not nearly as friendly or attractive—to escort Sawyer to the R & D wing. Sawyer gave the woman a wink as he walked away. Maybe a couple of months here wouldn't be so bad, after all.

The security guard led Sawyer down a series of hallways to a set of double doors. Sawyer watched as the man swiped a key-card through a scanner to unlock the door—adequate security, but not excellent and certainly not unbreakable—and opened it.

The Research & Development area was a much more open space than the hallway they had come through. It buzzed with activity, at least two dozen people working and talking at different stations and tables around the large room.

Another reception-type desk was near the door. The woman working here was not nearly as put-together as the graceful blonde at the Cyberdyne entrance. Here was a sort of mousy brunette with hair piled up in a messy bun at the top of her head and glasses perched on the edge of her nose. She didn't even acknowledge Sawyer and the guard as they entered the room—she was too busy rooting through a drawer.

Evidently she didn't find what she was looking for because she got up and walked over to a nearby filing cabinet and began searching through there.

Her gray pencil skirt and high-heeled black pumps with little bows made it difficult for Sawyer to stop staring at her legs. Wow. She might be mousy librarian on the top, but those legs… Sawyer noticed the security guard was also taking in the view.

When it became obvious the receptionist wasn't going to notice them, the security guard cleared his throat. "Excuse me, ma'am—"

The woman turned and took a few steps toward them. "Oh my goodness, I'm so sorry, Mark. You know me."

"It's no problem, ma'am." The guard's Southern accent was noticeable. He gestured toward Sawyer. "This is Agent Branson."

The receptionist glanced over at Sawyer, looking away before he could even smile at her. She turned back to the guard. "Thanks, Mark. We were expecting him. I'll take it from here."

The security guard smiled and nodded as he turned to leave—the man obviously had a little crush on the receptionist. Sawyer stepped forward to shake her hand and talk to her further, but she moved back.

"Can you give me a second? I'll be right with you." She didn't quite look him in the eye as she said it; her gaze never seemed to move past his chest.

Sawyer watched as the woman reopened the drawer in the filing cabinet and began rooting through it again. When the search proved fruitless, she moved to another drawer. She seemed to have forgotten Sawyer was even there. Sawyer just enjoyed the view of her legs until it seemed as if she might never come out.

"Did you lose something in there?" When the woman glanced up over her glasses, blinking at him with big round eyes, Sawyer offered her his most engaging smile.

She just continued to blink at him for a few moments, then shoved her head back into the search without saying a word.

Okay. Sawyer crossed his arms while watching her. He wasn't used to being ignored outright by women—especially cute little librarian ones with glasses, even though cute-librarian wasn't generally his type.

Of course, that didn't mean he couldn't still appreciate her. Sawyer could appreciate all women.

Eventually Cute Glasses found whatever it was she was looking for in the cavernous drawer—some sort of stain-remover stick or something. She gave a small sound of triumph and turned around. And seemed authentically surprised to see Sawyer standing there.

More blinks. "Um, yes. Agent Branson, right?"

Sawyer's eyebrows rose. "Forget I was here?" Sawyer shook his head with a half smile. She might be cute, but she was definitely the worst receptionist ever.

"I'm sorry, my mind tends to only focus on one thing at a time." She looked back up at him, again more at his general chest area than in the eyes. Meanwhile still blinking those big brown eyes of hers.

Maybe she was shy. Sawyer didn't mind shy and scatterbrained. Although the sophisticated beauty he met when he first entered the building was generally more his type, Sawyer certainly didn't mind spending a few minutes with shy, either. So he winked at her, when she finally peeked up at his eyes for a second, trying to put her at ease.

But that just seemed to throw her into more of a tizzy— she began reorganizing all the items on the desk—so Sawyer decided to just try to talk to her.

"So, I'm Sawyer Branson, the law-enforcement agent you were expecting. What's your name?"

"Megan." She was still clutching that stain-remover stick in one hand, moving office-supply products on the desk with the other.

"Have you worked here long?"

She looked at him oddly, then nodded. "About eight years."

Eight years? Wow, she must be somebody's relative or something if she was still this bad at her job after eight years. Sawyer smiled at her again—when he could catch her eye for a second—and leaned up against the desk. "That's great. Maybe if I have some questions about how things operate around here I can ask you about them."

Cute librarian Megan just nodded.

Sawyer looked around the open R & D area. People were

still working, although Sawyer noticed he and Megan had drawn some attention.

"I'm sure you know Dr. Fuller, right?" Sawyer asked in a conspiratorial tone. He might as well try to get as much information as he could before meeting the man.

That question certainly got Megan's attention—she finally looked him fully in the eye. "Oh." She said it with wonder as if some puzzle had just become clear to her. "You don't know who Dr. Fuller is." It wasn't a question.

"No, unfortunately, I was sent here without much information about him. Just that he needed protection while finishing a project for the government. As director of R & D, he would be your boss, right?"

Megan nodded. "Um, yes. Dr. Fuller is everyone's boss, I guess."

Sawyer smiled encouragingly; at least she was talking to him now. "Do you like him? Is he easy to get along with?"

Megan looked down and began moving items on the desk around again nervously. She obviously didn't want to answer his questions. That was fine. Sawyer didn't want to put her in a place where she had to speak badly about her boss. He decided to change the subject before Megan rearranged everything on her desk.

"Megan, do you think you could get me a cup of coffee somewhere or point me in the general direction of one? I'd just like to get some caffeine in my system before I meet Dr. Fuller."

Megan opened her mouth as if to answer him, but then just shut it again shaking her head. She seemed at an utter loss at what to say.

Cyberdyne really needed to look into replacing Megan as their R & D receptionist.

A man in a white lab coat, probably in his early forties, walked over to where Sawyer and Megan stood looking at each other. "Megan, is everything okay?" When Megan nodded, the man turned to Sawyer. "You must be Agent Branson. We were told you'd be arriving today. I'm Jonathan Bushman, Dr. Fuller's assistant."

Sawyer shook the man's outstretched hand. He decided not to mention the coffee; it had just been an attempt at changing the subject and he didn't want to get Megan in any sort of trouble.

"Great, Jonathan. I'm ready to meet Dr. Fuller whenever it's convenient."

Jonathan looked to Megan and then back to Sawyer, frowning. "But you already have." He gestured to Megan. "This is Dr. Zane Megan Fuller, lead conceptual and computer scientist for Cyberdyne."

OKAY, HAD THE federal agent just asked her to go get him some coffee? Megan had to admit he hadn't been obnoxious about it, but still…coffee? Of course, she couldn't really blame him. She had been puttering all around the desk, resorting back to her college behavior when she'd had no idea what to do when she was attracted to a member of the opposite gender—she'd practically lost her ability to speak for goodness' sake.

She had thought those days were long behind her, but evidently not when a man as gorgeous as Sawyer Branson talked to her. She could barely bring herself to meet his eyes for most of the conversation. He must have thought she was the worst secretary in the history of the world.

Megan had to remind herself that she was no longer that socially awkward, painfully shy sixteen-year-old girl she had been at MIT, intellectually ahead of all her classmates, but emotionally much less developed. Now Megan was twenty-nine years old, well respected and liked in her workplace and confident in her abilities and accolades.

If still a little shy socially.

Megan could see the wariness crossing Agent Branson's face as he realized his mistake. He probably wasn't too thrilled that he had asked her for a cup of coffee, either.

Megan stuck out her hand for him to shake. "Hi, I'm Dr. Fuller. Megan."

"Not the receptionist. I'm sorry about that." Megan could appreciate that Agent Branson had the good sense to at least look sheepish. His handshake was firm, and if Megan didn't know better she would almost swear she could feel his thumb caressing the back of her hand. That totally had to be her imagination. She pulled her hand back quickly.

"Yeah, there's not actually a receptionist for R & D, despite this desk. We just pretty much keep the desk as a catchall for office supplies and stuff." Megan held up the stain-remover stick. "I got a stain on my lab coat, so I was coming to see if I could use this to get it out."

Agent Branson nodded and gave her a half smile. "Well, a lab coat might have clued me in that you weren't a receptionist, but I definitely didn't know you were who I was here to see. My apologies."

Wow, if that was only a half smile, Megan didn't want to be around if he decided to turn his full charm on her. "I can still direct you to the coffee if you want it."

Agent Branson gave a bark of soft laughter. "Believe it or not, that was to make you feel more comfortable. You seemed to have lost the ability to speak for a while there."

Megan could feel a flush spilling over her. "Yeah, I definitely wouldn't have made a good receptionist. I'm more of a computer-person than a people-person."

Megan heard a throat clear from the other side of the desk. Jonathan. She had almost totally forgotten her assistant was there. Good Lord, she needed to focus. On the situation, not on Agent Branson.

"Jonathan, yes, okay. Um, Agent Branson, it sounds like you didn't know very much about me and we know even less about you. All we were told was that you would be 'a presence' here at Cyberdyne for a while. I don't really know why."

Agent Branson looked around. "Is there somewhere we could go to talk that isn't so open to everything?"

"Yes, of course. As you can see, we have an open workspace in general, but everyone also has offices. Mine is in the back." Megan began walking that way. "Should Jonathan join us?"

Agent Branson shook his head. "Right now, I'd just like it to be the two of us if that's okay. I'll need to talk with all of the R & D employees while I'm here, but I'd like to start with just you."

Megan could tell Jonathan didn't like that. But her assistant tended to be a little high-maintenance in that way. He always wanted to be involved with whatever was going on and tended to get a little churlish when he was left out. The behavior had been getting worse more recently. Megan tried to smile at Jonathan, but he had already turned away with a huff. Megan just shook her head and led Agent Branson back to her office, closing the door behind them.

Megan stood behind a chair at the table and gestured to another seat for Agent Branson. She couldn't help but admire the casual fluidity in how he filled the chair. As if he was a model.

If it wasn't for the scar on his chin and slightly crooked nose—it looked as though it had been broken at some point in his life—Agent Branson definitely could've made a living in front of the camera. Black hair, cut short and stylish, a perpetual five-o'clock shadow, gorgeous green eyes. Megan put a hand up to her chin just to make sure she wasn't accidentally drooling.

It was time to rein in all of this nonsense. Okay, yes, Agent Branson was attractive. Megan didn't know the specifics of exactly why he was here, but she did know that it wasn't for her ogling enjoyment. Megan took a deep breath in through her nose to focus herself, then released it gently through her mouth.

One of the advantages of being so intellectually advanced for her age when she was growing up—and always surrounded by older people —was that Megan had learned early how to act professionally even when she didn't feel that way. She wasn't going to let Agent Handsome discombobulate her any more than he already had today. She hoped they both would just totally forget the incident at the reception desk. That wasn't how she ran the R & D department—all flighty and unable to speak. She was a professional and she could handle this.

She could handle him.

Even though her lab coat had a small coffee stain on it, Megan grabbed it from where it hung on a hook on the back of her door and put it on. She immediately felt more secure with its familiar weight on her shoulders. She sat down and looked across the table.

"So, Agent Branson, how can we help you here at Cyberdyne?"

Evidently she had succeeded in adding the desired professionalism to her tone as she watched Agent Branson sit up a little straighter in his chair, his eyes narrowing slightly for just a moment. Obviously he was also expecting the nervous woman he had met earlier at the desk.

Well, she wasn't around anymore.

Chapter Three

Sawyer watched pretty Megan transform into stuffy, prickly Dr. Zane Megan Fuller—just like her name tag said—as she pulled on that drab lab coat and buttoned it. The skirt underneath, and evidently the shy woman from the desk, disappeared. Sawyer could almost feel the temperature drop around him.

Okay, the asking her for coffee had been a bit of a misstep. Sawyer totally read that situation wrong—not something he was used to doing. He tried to think back to his conversation with Burgamy. Sawyer definitely would've remembered if his boss had said Dr. Fuller was an attractive young woman. Or if he had said *woman* at all.

What had Sawyer been expecting in Dr. Fuller again? Someone balding, with thick glasses and a bow tie? Sawyer could admit he'd let a stereotype get the better of him. It was his own fault and he knew better. But when he'd seen pretty little Megan fumbling around at the desk, blinking up at him with those big brown eyes and blushing for goodness' sake?

It had never even crossed Sawyer's mind that she would be the head computer scientist of a multimillion-dollar company. But the woman sitting across from him so coldly, lab coat around her like a suit of armor? He had no problem picturing her as Dr. Fuller, brilliant scientist.

"Yes, Dr. Fuller. I'm sorry for the confusion before." Reflexively Sawyer tried to smile at her, but he was met only with cold professionalism. "I've been sent here from the Bureau to discuss Ghost Shell."

Sawyer knew Megan would associate the word *bureau* with the FBI, but now wasn't the time to explain about Omega Sector. Omega was a task force made up of representatives from all different sorts of government agencies—FBI, CIA, Homeland Security, hell, even Interpol—who answered to bosses inside Omega. The task force was generally kept on a need-to-know basis. All Megan needed to know right now was that Sawyer was from federal law enforcement.

Megan nodded curtly. "I gave Ghost Shell to the FBI three months ago. Then I receive a follow-up call a few days ago with all sorts of questions you guys should already know the answer to."

Sawyer didn't respond to that directly. "I understand you've been working on a countermeasure to Ghost Shell."

That obviously wasn't the statement she was expecting. "Well, we were. But once I turned Ghost Shell over to the FBI, we put that on the back burner. Didn't seem important to work on the antidote for a poison we'd already gotten rid of."

"Unfortunately, it looks like the poison is back."

"What?" Her big brown eyes blinked at him again, but this time with confusion rather than shyness.

"Ghost Shell fell into the wrong hands not long ago."

"What?" Megan parroted herself. "I gave Ghost Shell to the FBI to keep that exact thing from happening."

Sawyer grimaced. "I understand your frustration."

Sawyer watched Megan's small fists ball on the table. He slid back a little in his chair, since it looked as if she might start swinging any moment. Not that he could blame her.

"My research team here at Cyberdyne put in hundreds

of man-hours on Ghost Shell! The work we did was brilliant and could've potentially made Cyberdyne millions of dollars. But I chose—my *team* chose—to stop our progress when we realized how easily Ghost Shell could become a weapon." One of her small fists came down forcefully on the table. "And now you're telling me some terrorist group has it anyway?"

"Well, yes and no."

One eyebrow rose. "I think perhaps you should just cut to the chase, Agent Branson."

Totally gone was the shy, stammering woman he had seen at the front desk. This woman in front of him—he definitely could not think of her as mousy in any way—was a force to be reckoned with.

"The agent in charge of the technology you gave the FBI—"

"Fred McNeil."

Sawyer shouldn't be surprised that Megan remembered the name of an agent she'd spoken to months before, given her reputation. "Yes, Fred McNeil. Ends up he was also working for a crime-syndicate group known as DS-13."

Megan closed her eyes and shook her head, her breath coming out in a hiss. "And is this DS-13 group terrorists?"

"No. But they would not hesitate to sell Ghost Shell to whatever terrorist faction was willing to pay the highest price."

"And now DS-13 has Ghost Shell."

"Again, yes and no." Sawyer held his hand out to stop the sound of exasperation he knew was coming. "In a mission two weeks ago, one version—the working version—of Ghost Shell was recovered. But until we contacted you just a couple of days ago, we had no idea a second version of Ghost Shell even existed."

"But you don't have the other version?"

"No, Fred McNeil is still at large with it."

Megan got up and began pacing around her office. "The other version, although not as dangerous as the first, is still definitely not benign. It's just as potentially dangerous."

"But it would take someone with a special set of skills to complete it, right?"

Megan shrugged a delicate shoulder. "My ego would like to think so. But really, anybody skilled in reverse engineering—taking something apart and figuring out what makes it work—and software development could probably do it. There's a dozen people at Cyberdyne alone."

"So the FBI should be acting on the assumption that Fred McNeil and DS-13 could have a working prototype at any time."

Megan took off her glasses and rubbed her eyes, leaning back against her desk. "Absolutely. With the right help, it won't take long."

"We're going to do everything we can to stop that from happening."

"No offense, Agent Branson, but my trusting the FBI is how this whole problem happened in the first place."

Sawyer grimaced. There really wasn't much argument around that one. "On behalf of the entire Bureau, I want to apologize for what happened. Nobody had any idea that Fred McNeil had flipped."

"Well, thanks for the apology, but that doesn't necessarily make me feel much better." The ice doctor was back in full force. "Did you work with Agent McNeil?"

"No. I'm in an entirely different…section of the Bureau. Never met the man."

"How do I know I can trust you?"

"Well, for one thing, I'm bringing Ghost Shell *back* to you, not the other way around. But also, there's a whole department involved this time. Not just one person. A lot more accountability that way."

Megan stared at him for a long moment. "I guess so. Fred

McNeil always seemed to want to keep things so quiet and just between us. Now I know why." Megan shuddered. "He was so smarmy. I should've known better."

"We're working around-the-clock to find McNeil and Ghost Shell before it can be developed more fully."

"What exactly do you want from us here at Cyberdyne?"

"We need you to finish the countermeasure decryption system you were working on before."

Megan shook her head and sat back down at the table. "I explained to whoever I talked to a couple of days ago that I can't do it without Ghost Shell. That's why I stopped working on it months ago."

"I have the first version of Ghost Shell with me. I know you will need this version to create the countermeasure so we can stop McNeil once he gets his version of Ghost Shell up and running."

"You have Ghost Shell here, unguarded?" Megan stood back up. "Then we need to get that drive into the vault right away. It's too valuable, too dangerous for you to just be casually carrying it around."

Sawyer tried not to be offended. "I think I'm capable of guarding a software system for a few hours, Dr. Fuller."

It looked as if Megan would argue the point further, but then decided to let it go. "Fine. But you'll have to excuse me for not having too much faith in FBI agents at the current moment. And, honestly, why shouldn't I just wash my hands of this entire thing? My team and I did our job right. It's you guys who messed things up."

Sawyer took a breath. He needed to convince Megan to help them. Because if she decided she'd already done her part, and that law enforcement were on their own, Omega's job was about to become a lot harder.

Sawyer looked at Megan, who was standing beside her desk, lips pressed into a white slash, posture rigid. He couldn't blame her for how she was feeling.

But they needed her help, and right now it didn't look as though she was very interested in giving it.

Sawyer knew his colleagues considered him to be the charming Branson brother; they teased him about it all the time back at Omega. People—and okay, he could admit it, women especially—responded to him. It was a gift, and Sawyer had used it to his advantage multiple times in different operations. It made undercover work a natural fit— who didn't want to like the guy with the easy smile and quick joke? But his easy smile didn't seem to be getting him anywhere in this conversation, not since the ice doctor had appeared.

It was amazing how different this controlled woman was from the pretty librarian-type he'd talked to at the desk. The woman at the desk Sawyer would've known how to reach, even with her shyness. Yet this woman didn't seem to see him as a man—hell, even as a person—at all. But he had to try to get her cooperation.

"You're right, the FBI has messed things up." Sawyer smiled and held a hand out to her in a gesture for her to sit back down. Standing up and towering over her wasn't the way to make her feel more comfortable. "And Fred McNeil fooled a lot of people, not just you."

Sawyer noticed Megan's posture slump slightly. Evidently McNeil's ability to fool her weighed more heavily on Megan than she wanted to admit.

Sawyer continued, "I don't have to tell you how important it is that Ghost Shell not fall into the hands of terrorists. *You're* the one who came to us with the problem because you could see the catastrophic damage Ghost Shell was capable of. Without you, law enforcement would have no idea of the potential threat they were up against."

He reached out and touched her hand that rested on the table. "Thank you for coming forward. I'm pretty sure nobody has said that to you, but somebody should have."

For a moment, looking into her big brown eyes, Sawyer saw Megan, not the cold Dr. Fuller. Sawyer realized maybe it had been *him* not seeing her as a person, not vice versa. Dr. Fuller and Megan were one and the same; he needed to remember that. Sawyer squeezed her hand in a friendly manner, then let her go.

"You're good at what you do," Megan said after a moment.

"And what's that?"

"Manipulating people."

Sawyer shook his head. "I know it seems that way, but I'm not trying to manipulate you, I promise. Everything I've said so far has been the absolute truth."

She looked at him with one eyebrow raised, but seemed to have lost a little of her coldness, so Sawyer continued, "But don't get me wrong, I'm definitely asking you for something. We need your help. We've got to have a way to stop Ghost Shell when DS-13 goes to sell their version on the black market. You are our best hope for that."

Megan sighed, resignation clear in her eyes. "All right, Agent Branson. Whether you're trying to deliberately manipulate me or not, I guess you're going to get what you want. I'll get the Ghost Shell countermeasure finished as soon as possible." Megan stood up again and wiped an imaginary piece of lint off her lab coat. "But I'm not doing it for you. I'm doing it because it's the right thing to do. I just hope you guys don't screw it up again."

"I'll make you a deal. You get the Ghost Shell countermeasure completed and I will personally make sure nobody on my end of things screws it up." Agent Branson had such utter confidence in his voice that Megan couldn't help but believe him.

Megan couldn't sit there and say she wasn't affected by Agent Branson. But it wasn't as if he was trying to talk her into going out with him; he was trying to get Megan to do something she was already willing to do.

Not that she wasn't willing to go out with him.

But not that he was asking.

Megan had to get herself under control. Him asking or not asking her out was not the issue here. Ghost Shell and saving the world was. *Focus. Be professional.*

"So should I announce the change in projects to everyone?"

Agent Branson shook his head. "No, we want to keep this to as few people as possible."

Megan nodded. That was probably best. Although she trusted everyone who worked in the R & D department, the fewer people who knew about all this, the better. "Okay, just my inner team then. That's seven people including me and Jonathan Bushman, my assistant, whom you met."

"That sounds good."

"Great. So I guess I'll call you in a couple of weeks when we have the countermeasure completed." Megan stuck out her hand to shake his. The sooner she got him out of her office, the sooner she could focus on other things. *Any* other thing besides his presence here.

"Actually, I'll be staying here for a while if that's okay."

"For the meeting with the team? That's probably a good idea." Her inner team rarely needed to be more focused than they already were, but Agent Branson could provide added motivation to get the Ghost Shell countermeasure completed faster.

"No. I'll be staying until you're finished."

"The whole time? You know, this isn't going to be done in a day. It's going to take a while. Plus, we are a secure facility, especially within the R & D vault. You can leave Ghost Shell here and come back in a couple of weeks. I promise it will be safe."

"Even so, I'll be staying."

This was not good. Having him here was going to wreak havoc on her concentration. "It'll be pretty boring. You understand that, right?"

Megan watched Sawyer's brows furrow as he nodded curtly, with no enthusiasm whatsoever. Evidently, he didn't really want to be here. Megan wasn't surprised; watching a group of scientists do conceptual engineering for days or weeks did not strike Megan as something a man like Sawyer would want to do on his own accord.

"Drew the short straw, huh?" she asked him.

Megan could tell she had surprised him. He laughed, then looked down at her with his megawatt smile. "Something like that," he finally said. "Maybe I'll tell you about it sometime while I'm here. You'll like that story."

Megan seemed to have forgotten how to breathe at his smile. She finally forced herself to look away and grabbed all the folders on her desk—most of them ones she didn't even need—and called her inner team to the conference room for a meeting.

This group of people had developed Ghost Shell at one stage or another and was well aware of its potentials and dangers. Without going into the details about what had happened with Fred McNeil and DS-13, Megan explained that developing the countermeasure to Ghost Shell had become a priority for them at Cyberdyne.

Sawyer's presence in the room couldn't be ignored, so Megan introduced him.

"This is Agent Sawyer Branson. He'll be here for the duration of the project. The fact that law enforcement feels his presence here is necessary should be a reminder of how crucial this project is."

Two of the women on the team—both in their midforties and both married with children—were all but ogling Sawyer. Megan resisted the urge to rap something against the conference table to get their attention.

Branson seemed to be taking it all in stride, smiling easily at the women. Of course, he smiled easily at the men, too. He just seemed to have a way that put everyone at ease.

Everyone except Megan.

Megan dismissed the meeting a little more curtly than she had planned, after they all agreed work would begin first thing in the morning. She left the conference room without waiting to see if Agent Branson was coming with her or not. If he wanted to flirt with everyone in the department, that was his business. As long as it didn't interfere with their work, Megan had absolutely no problem with it.

Good to see that the FBI had once again sent their very best.

Megan knew she was being unreasonable. What the heck was wrong with her? She sat down and rested for a minute. It had been a long day, made more stressful by the bad news Sawyer had delivered. She had been such an idiot to trust Fred McNeil. Even though Sawyer told her McNeil had fooled everyone, Megan knew she should've trusted her instincts with McNeil.

But Megan had never been good at trusting her instincts unless it came to science. Trusting her instincts with men had always brought her a heartache or headache.

Megan rubbed at a knot that was beginning to form in her neck. She took a deep breath and began reorganizing all the mostly unneeded files she had taken to the meeting back into their rightful places on her desk. Then she cleared off and straightened any other items that cluttered it or were out of place. She knew that a clean desk always made her feel better and would help her when she got to work tomorrow with a new, stressful agent on her hands.

Project. New, stressful *project* on her hands, damn it.

And speak of the devil… Agent Branson was making his way over to her office. He rapped on the outside of her office door, but entered without waiting for an invite.

"Get to meet everyone on the team?" It was the most neutral question Megan could think of.

"Yep. Seems like a pretty solid crew you have there." He looked around her office. "And looks like you've got that desk of yours about as pristine as they come."

Megan shrugged and smiled ruefully. "Having everything neat and organized helps me work. It'll help me focus when I get back to work in the morning. But right now I'm going to head home and have a nice glass of wine. How about you?"

Megan watched as Sawyer's head tilted to the side and he raised one eyebrow. "Sure. I mean, I don't know you very well, but I'd like to have a glass of wine at your house."

Megan could've bitten off her own tongue. He thought she was asking him out? No. He absolutely could not come over to her house for a glass of wine. She could barely form coherent sentences around him here. She definitely didn't want him in her home.

"No. I mean—I wasn't asking you over. I don't want you to come over to my house. I just meant—" Megan stopped herself—she was just making it worse.

"Oh, well, then, we could go out to a bar or restaurant or something." Sawyer's eyes were lit with amusement as he said it. "Just let me grab my stuff."

"No! I don't want to go out with you. I just want to go home by myself." It sounded rude even to her own ears.

Sawyer chuckled. "I know what you meant, Megan. I was just giving you a hard time."

Megan didn't know what to say. She just grabbed her purse from the back of the office door and left without another word. She was probably coming across as childish, but didn't care. His charming laughter followed her down the hall.

How was she ever going to make it through the next few weeks with Sawyer Branson around her all the time?

Chapter Four

Arriving back at Megan's office at Cyberdyne first thing the next morning, Sawyer was determined not to tease her about the incident the night before. But he had to admit it was tempting. So tempting.

And icy Dr. Fuller was back in full force this morning. Sawyer could tell as soon as he walked in the door.

"Agent Branson," Megan said with a brief nod. "Good morning."

So they were back to Agent Branson. "And to you, Dr. Fuller," Sawyer responded in the same formal tone. Megan's eyes narrowed at that, as if she couldn't decide if he was mocking her or not. That was okay; Sawyer couldn't decide if he was mocking her, either.

"Is it all right if I put my things in here or would you prefer me somewhere else?" Sawyer asked her. He didn't have much—but he needed somewhere to set up his laptop and files. He didn't want to be totally useless while he was here; there were at least some things he could accomplish on the computer while babysitting.

Sawyer just hoped Megan's team would be able to construct the countermeasure quickly so he could get back to Omega as soon as possible.

"Here is fine. I'll just clear off the table for you." She

moved a few files from the table, then nodded curtly again. "There you go, Agent Branson."

"Megan, I thought that since you asked me out last night you could at least call me Sawyer." So much for his resolution not to tease her.

He could almost physically see the heat suffusing her face. "About that, um—" Megan wasn't looking in Sawyer's eyes, but he could tell she was at least forcing herself to hold still and not fidget. "I apologize. My words didn't come out correctly last night and then I didn't handle the situation well."

Now Sawyer felt bad. He had thought it was kind of cute the way she had gotten so discombobulated, but she obviously was berating herself for the behavior. "Megan, I was just kidding. Don't worry about it—"

"I behaved childishly."

"You didn't behave childishly. I deliberately misconstrued what you said and I shouldn't have. I knew the entire time you weren't asking me out. I should be the one apologizing, not you."

Megan finally looked up at him. "Fine. I accept your almost-apology, Agent Branson."

"Thank you, Dr. Fuller. But I do wish you'd call me Sawyer."

Sawyer wasn't sure if Megan was about to agree or argue the point when one of the lab technicians came flying into her office.

"Dr. Fuller, we have a huge problem in the vault. We need you to come right away."

A flash of relief crossed Megan's face before it was drowned out by concern. She turned and hurried out of her office without another word. Sawyer followed right behind her.

Obviously the lab tech's definition of *huge problem* and

Sawyer's differed greatly, Sawyer realized. There was no smoke here in the vault, no bullets, no blood.

The Cyberdyne R & D vault wasn't a vault like that of a bank. Instead it was just a secure area, with a further locked door and a higher security clearance needed to enter. No stranger could just wander around any part of Cyberdyne from off the street; everyone was escorted by someone. Beyond that, only certain people were cleared to enter the R & D department. From what Sawyer could tell, it looked as if everyone had their own key-card that tracked who came and left out of the general R & D department.

"The vault holds our more highly classified or secretive items," Megan explained as they entered the secure room. "But really, it's more of a safe place to store items than anything else."

"Who has access?"

"Me and select members of the R & D team. And security guards, I guess."

That was good. Limited access definitely made any area more secure. Sawyer made a mental note to get to know the head of Cyberdyne security.

"We don't really use the vault to keep out thieves or anything like that," Megan continued. "It's more to keep important items safe from a much more treacherous enemy—human error. When you've got multiple people walking around day in and day out you're bound to have spills, misplacements or other accidents. The vault is primarily to save important items from those sorts of problems."

Jonathan Bushman, Megan's assistant, was sitting with rigid posture in front of a computer station in the vault.

"What's going on, Jon?" Megan walked over to stand right beside him.

"It's the hard drive that housed the Ghost Shell countermeasure. It's critically damaged."

Megan pulled her glasses from the top of her head to get a better look at the drive. "What? It was fine the last time I accessed it."

Sawyer walked over closer to the two of them. "When was that?"

"I don't know, maybe eight weeks ago? We can check the logs to find out exactly." She said all this without looking at Sawyer. "Can you recover anything, Jon?"

"Nothing useful." Jon spoke with a heavy sigh.

Megan picked up the drive and held it in her hands like a wounded bird. Sawyer noticed some scratches on the outside of it.

"See those scratches? Do you think it was external damage that caused the problem? Or is it more internal issues?" Sawyer asked.

Jonathan just rolled his eyes and went back to scanning the screen looking for any recoverable data. Megan turned to Sawyer. "Something happening to it externally could certainly cause damage, if someone, say, stepped on the drive or put something heavy on top of it."

Sawyer nodded. "Could something internally have been done to it deliberately to make the data unrecoverable?"

Both Jonathan and Megan turned to look at Sawyer sharply. "Like some sort of sabotage?" Jonathan asked.

Sawyer shrugged. "It happens."

Jonathan was obviously about to take offense. Megan leaned back against the computer station so she was face-to-face with Sawyer. She put her hand on Jonathan's shoulder.

"I'm pretty sure we don't have anyone working here who would do anything like that. Especially not anyone who has access to the vault."

Jonathan nodded vigorously.

"But there's no way of telling when the damage was done?" Sawyer asked.

Megan shook her head. "No. It could've sat here damaged for weeks."

"Or it could've been damaged last night or this morning after you announced the team would begin working on
the countermeasure."

Megan sighed. "Yes, Agent Branson. It is possible it
happened within the last twenty-four hours. But I doubt it."

Sawyer decided not to push it since they had no way of
knowing when the damage had occurred. "Do things get
damaged in here often?"

"Not often, but it has happened. It happens more often
out there." Megan gestured vaguely with a hand toward
the general R & D area. Then she turned and refocused on
the screen in front of Jonathan. Within moments they were
in a deep discussion about what, if anything, could be salvaged. Neither looked very optimistic.

Sawyer stepped back and looked around the vault.
There were cabinets and shelves of varying size. Everything seemed highly organized and labeled—via Megan's
decree he was sure. Nothing lay around haphazardly or
seemed to be damaged as far as Sawyer could tell. Like
Megan had told him, the vault was equipped to protect its
items from human accidents and mistakes. It seemed to
do that very well.

Except for in this one case. Sawyer couldn't help but be
suspicious of that.

His phone buzzed in his pocket. Evan Karcz. Good,
maybe now Sawyer could get an update on what was happening back at Omega.

Sawyer walked out of the vault without saying anything
to Megan and Jonathan. They were obviously deeply focused on the countermeasure salvage. Sawyer doubted they
would miss him at all.

"Evan. How's it going in the real world?"

Evan chuckled a little at Sawyer's greeting. "I take it that means you're still less than thrilled with your Cyberdyne assignment?"

"Well, let's just say it hasn't been what I expected."

"Oh yeah? More interesting or less?"

Sawyer glanced over his shoulder at Megan before walking farther down the hall toward her office. "More interesting. Definitely more."

That got Evan's attention. "Is something happening there, Sawyer? Good news, I hope."

"Dr. Fuller thought it was going to take up to a few weeks to finish the Ghost Shell countermeasure, but we encountered a setback first thing this morning." Sawyer told Evan about the problem in the vault.

"Well, that's definitely not good. I hope they can recover something from the drive, because things are going to hell in a handbasket around here concerning DS-13 and Fred McNeil."

"Movement?" Sawyer proceeded all the way into Megan's office and closed the door.

"Word is, DS-13 is going to have some sort of infiltrative software system coming available in the next couple of weeks."

"That sounds exactly like Ghost Shell."

"I thought so, too."

"Dr. Fuller said there were a number of computer people who would be able to finish the work on their version of Ghost Shell. That it was only a matter of time."

"He was right, it looks like."

Sawyer decided to let the erroneous pronoun choice go for the time being. "So what's the plan?"

"I'm still going under. But as Bob Sinclair."

That stopped Sawyer in his tracks. "What?"

"I know, Sawyer, believe me, I know. But one of my

contacts who has direct ties with DS-13 reached out to me as Bob Sinclair about all this Ghost Shell mess."

"I thought you retired Bob Sinclair a year ago. After…" Sawyer couldn't even bring himself to say it.

Bob Sinclair was an undercover persona Evan had carefully developed as a high-end weapons buyer for terrorist groups. Juliet, Sawyer's sister, had gone undercover with him as Lisa Sinclair, Bob's wife. Until it had ended in tragedy.

"Sawyer, I know what you're thinking. And believe me, Juliet won't be involved this time."

"She better the hell not be, Evan. She's not ready."

"Nobody wants to protect Juliet more than me."

"Fine, just leave her out of it. And make sure Burgamy isn't putting any pressure on her to go back under, either." Sawyer didn't like being away from Omega where he could make sure for himself that his sister wasn't being pressured to go back undercover. But he trusted Evan.

"I just wanted you to know what was going on. Word is to expect a big sale coming up in the next couple of weeks. If that's Ghost Shell, we need to be ready with the countermeasure."

"Roger that. Dr. Fuller was pretty pissed off about what happened with Fred McNeil. Took a bit of convincing to get the team to trust that I wasn't going to do something similar and get working on the countermeasure."

Evan chuckled. "Dr. Fuller giving you hell? Even after only one day?"

"Yeah, she's something."

"She? I thought it was Dr. *Zane* Fuller?"

"Yeah, Dr. Zane *Megan* Fuller. Not sure if Burgamy left out the Megan part on accident or on purpose." Sawyer rolled his eyes.

"Well, I certainly imagined that wrong. I guess two degrees from MIT made me think middle-aged guy."

"You're not the only one. But try female in her late twenties."

Sawyer had to pull his phone back from his ear, Evan was laughing so hard. "Of course she is."

"Shut up, Evan."

"Look, I'll let you go play with your scientist, but tell her to hurry up with the countermeasure." Somberness crept back into Evan's tone. "It's going to be easy for this situation to get shot straight to hell very quickly."

"I know, man, you be careful. Your Bob Sinclair cover has some holes, especially without Juliet."

"Don't worry, I'll get it worked out. Looks like I might be coming down toward your current location. My contact is not far out of Asheville."

DS-13 with movement just outside Asheville? Another interesting coincidence Sawyer wasn't going to take at face value.

Sawyer saw Megan walking toward the office from the vault. "All right, man. Keep me posted if anything further develops. As soon as Cyberdyne has the countermeasure completed, you'll be my first call."

Megan tapped lightly on the door before walking in just as Sawyer was ending the call.

"How'd it go?" Sawyer asked her.

Megan threw the file she was carrying down on her desk. "I hope that whoever you were talking to had some good news for you. Because after a complete scan of the damaged hard drive, we discovered that almost nothing is recoverable. We're basically starting from scratch."

Chapter Five

Four days later, Megan was considering killing herself and everyone around her. Absolutely nothing was going right with the Ghost Shell countermeasure. Everything she and the team did seemed to be one-step-forward and two-steps-back. First having to start from scratch after the drive was damaged, then errors both human and mechanical plagued them.

She was one mistake away from becoming a homicidal maniac.

Megan was used to working under pressure. Pressure was a challenge she generally enjoyed—it forced her brain to exert in ways not normally required of it. Thinking faster often produced new and exciting solutions that working a problem slowly often missed.

But right now thinking faster was just producing a bunch of junk.

Admittedly, the pressure Megan usually fell under wasn't the save-the-world variety. It tended to be more of the save money or time variety. Knowing that if they didn't get the countermeasure completed before Ghost Shell was sold on the black market by this DS-13 group then thousands of lives could be lost tended to put Megan a little on edge.

But really it was Sawyer Branson's constant presence

here that was damaging Megan's calm. Not that he was critical or did anything to deliberately make her uncomfortable, he was just always *there*. Observing, reporting, ready to help if there was anything he could do.

It was driving her absolutely nuts.

After yet another error in the computer coding had forced Megan's team to backtrack again this morning, Megan had decided to leave them to that part and take an early working lunch.

And yeah, Megan could admit she was hiding out a little from Sawyer here in the small break room of the R & D department.

She had brought with her the new drive she and the team had partially rebuilt over the past couple of days. Her lunch tote was stuffed with printouts concerning the source code and combinatorial algorithms needed for the project, as well as a ham-and-cheese sandwich. Megan hoped she could get some work done in here. Almost everybody used the larger companywide cafeteria to eat rather than this small break room. Blessed quiet reigned here.

Halfway through her sandwich and the printouts Megan heard the door open. She didn't look up from her work, hoping whoever entered either wasn't looking for her or would see she was busy and not disturb her. A few moments of silence reassured her.

"You're cute when you concentrate really hard like that."

Sawyer. Almost instantly the words Megan had been concentrating on became gibberish on the printout in front of her. She just couldn't think when he was around.

"I'm working." Megan knew she was being borderline rude, again, but couldn't help it. Acting cold around him was the only way not to become a babbling idiot like she had been on the first day.

"I see that. Mind if I hang out in here for a while? I'll be quiet, I promise."

Yes, Megan minded. His very presence in the room bothered her. Everything about him bothered her. "Fine."

True to his word Sawyer didn't say anything else, not
even to point out how rude Megan was being, but it didn't
seem to matter. Try as she might, Megan couldn't get any
work done with Sawyer around. When she found herself
reading the same page for the third time, she decided she'd
had enough. She was going home.

Megan stood up and began cramming stuff into bags.
She realized she had put the remaining part of her sandwich in her briefcase and the Ghost Shell drive in her lunch
bag, but she didn't care.

Sawyer watched calmly from his table near the door.
"Finished with lunch?"

"I can't work in here anymore. There's too much noise."

Sawyer looked around as if to discover what noise she
referred to. Megan couldn't blame him. Except for the
sound of Megan frantically stuffing papers into whatever
bag happened to be closest, it was completely silent in the
break room.

"I'm going home to work for the rest of the afternoon."
Megan couldn't afford to lose another whole day, no matter what the reason. Especially because of her own ridicu-
lousness. There was too much at stake.

Megan took her bags and marched out of the break room,
without looking at or speaking to Sawyer, and headed toward her office. Jonathan and the rest of the team were sitting around one of the conference tables in the middle of
the main R & D room looking much more relieved than
when she had left them this morning. Jonathan stood when
he saw Megan, a report in hand.

"Megan, it looks like we figured out the coding problem.
Well, it was mostly Trish." Jonathan gestured to the woman
next to him. "Now we just have to finish it."

"Great, you guys. I'm going to be working off-site this

afternoon, so I need you all to get this done so we can start fresh tomorrow. Hopefully, I'll have some of our other Ghost Shell problems worked out by then."

Megan encouraged everyone a bit more, then headed back to her office. Jonathan followed her, along with Trish, one of the newer Cyberdyne team members, who always seemed to be trying to get more face time with Megan.

"Where are you going to be this afternoon?" Jonathan asked Megan.

"Just off-site somewhere, probably at home. I need to get away from Cyberdyne for a little while so I can think clearly. Everything here is holding me back."

Megan noticed Jonathan's pinched features. Great, now she had hurt her assistant's pride. "Jon, you know how I am. Sometimes I just need to be away from everything to break through a problem." Megan turned to include Trish in the conversation. "If you two can get the coding finished, then tomorrow we can meet back here and really make some progress."

Jonathan finally nodded. "Okay, I guess you're right. Is Agent Branson going with you?"

Megan looked up and saw Sawyer walking toward them from the break room. "No, Agent Branson will definitely be staying here. Otherwise it will defeat the entire purpose."

Trish nodded as if she totally understood what Megan was saying. Megan just grimaced. Another woman under Sawyer's spell did not make Megan feel any better.

Jonathan gestured down to Megan's briefcase. "Do you have everything you need? Do you want anything we were working on this morning? I can get it for you."

"No, I think I'm okay. I've got the printouts and hard drive. That should be all I need. We're close, you guys, I can feel it."

Trish nodded. "I know. It feels good, doesn't it? To actually make forward progress? It seemed like the fates have conspired against us the last few days."

"Well, let's hope that's all behind us now."

Sawyer stopped outside her office and tapped on the door. "Can I speak to you for a minute, Megan?"

"Yes." Megan turned to Jonathan. "I'll see you tomorrow, Trish, Jon. Okay? Thanks for your help."

Both computer scientists nodded and left, already discussing the coding problem. Megan was thankful to have team members who were so dedicated to what they did.

"You're really going to work somewhere else today?"

Megan began unbuttoning her lab coat. "Yes. Believe it or not, it happens. Sometimes I need to be in a different element in order to break through a problem. It's just how my brain works." She turned her back to him to slip off the coat.

"I'll come with you."

"No!" Megan took a deep breath and then spun back slowly to face Sawyer. "I mean, that's not necessary. Thanks." Megan could tell Sawyer was about to argue, so she continued, "Sawyer, thank you for the offer, but I really just need to be alone. Otherwise I won't be able to get the work done."

"I'm not sure it's a good idea for you to be off on your own."

"I'm just going to my house, Sawyer. It's a chance for me to get in multiple uninterrupted hours of work. If I'm here, there's always someone who needs me for something or other distractions." Megan couldn't look at Sawyer's face as she finished the sentence, so she turned to her desk and began grabbing her bags.

"Fine." Megan was a little surprised to hear Sawyer say it. She thought she was going to have to present further arguments for why he couldn't come with her. And to be honest she wasn't sure what those arguments would be.

Sorry, Sawyer, you can't come with me because when-

*ever you're around I can't seem to focus on anything but how...*yummy *you look.*

Sawyer had been nothing but polite and friendly to Megan over the past few days—just like he had been to everyone. This craziness was all in Megan's head, not in his actions.

"Give me your phone," Sawyer told her. "So I can put my number in it."

Megan gave it to him and he continued, "If you have any issues, call me. Or if you decide to go anywhere but your house, let me know."

"Okay."

"I'm going to stay here because there are a couple of concerns I want to look into."

"About Ghost Shell?"

"Yes. But I'm not certain about anything yet, so don't worry about it now. We'll talk tomorrow when you get back. Right now the most important thing is that you get some real progress made with the countermeasure."

Megan agreed. "I know. I work best alone."

"That's the main reason I'm letting you go alone. I know you don't really like me around when you're working, Megan. I annoy you. That's fine." Sawyer smiled and winked. "My manly ego can take it, I think."

He thought she didn't want him around because she didn't like him? Obviously he couldn't see how her pulse started racing when he smiled at her. Better to keep it that way.

"Well, I'm sure you never lack for female company of those you don't annoy."

"I am highly suspicious of any woman who isn't annoyed by me." Sawyer winked at Megan.

She grabbed her stuff and headed toward the door without another word before she hyperventilated. She heard Sawyer chuckle as she brushed past him.

"See you tomorrow, Dr. Fuller," he called as she walked down the hall. Megan didn't respond. What could she say anyway?

Megan made her way down the hallway, reporting to Mark, the main security guard, that she was leaving for the day to work at home and would be back tomorrow.

When Mark smiled at her it didn't do anything to her stomach. She smiled back as he helped her with the front door.

The crisp winter air felt good against Megan's overheated skin. She walked slowly to her car enjoying—as always—the beauty of the Blue Ridge Mountains surrounding her. Here, outside and away from all the craziness inside Cyberdyne and her reaction to Sawyer, Megan realized she had made the right decision.

She already felt clearer, steadier. Ready to work. What she was doing was important and she was racing against a very real clock, but she was up for the challenge. Working at home would be just what she needed.

Megan opened her car door and threw her briefcase and lunch bag in the passenger seat beside her. Her house was only ten minutes away from Cyberdyne. She'd chosen it specifically for that reason. She cleared through the security gate and began her drive home.

As she stopped at an intersection about halfway between her house and Cyberdyne, an idea for solving one of the problems with the countermeasure became clear to Megan. She reached into her purse to grab her phone so she could make a voice recording, to remember it later.

A car behind her honked as Megan was getting her phone ready to record. The light had turned green. Megan waved to the car behind her and began to pull through the intersection.

Just as an SUV flew through the intersection in the other direction and T-boned into the passenger side of Megan's car.

Chapter Six

The jar of the impact threw Megan's entire body into the driver's side door. Her head cracked against the window and she struggled to hold on to consciousness. Her car seemed to spin around in slow motion from the force of the SUV that hit it.

Megan sat dazed as the car stopped moving, trying to figure out what exactly had happened. Thinking was hard. Had the other car run the red light? Megan tried to test different parts of her body to make sure they were functional, thankful that everything seemed to move when her brain commanded it to.

Was everyone all right in the other car? Megan reached up to wipe the sweat trickling from her scalp, but when she brought her fingers down they were red. Blood, not sweat.

Megan tried to unfasten her seat belt, but it didn't seem to want to come loose. She glanced out the window and saw someone from the SUV that had hit her get out of the passenger side of their vehicle and begin walking toward her car. Thank goodness he seemed to be okay. Megan hoped the driver was, too.

And that they had insurance.

The man hurried up to Megan's car and leaned into the passenger-side window that had completely shattered.

"Oh my gosh." Megan's words came out in a rush. "Are

you guys okay? My seat belt seems to be stuck. And I think I'm bleeding. I might need an ambulance, but I think over-all I'm okay."

The man didn't say anything, and Megan couldn't tell if he was injured or not. He was wearing a gray jersey jacket with a hood tied tightly around his face. And with the large, dark sunglasses he had on, Megan couldn't tell anything about him at all.

The hooded man reached down and grabbed Megan's briefcase that had slid to the floor during the impact. He stretched toward her and, in her dazed state, Megan thought he might try to help her with her seat belt. But then she realized he was trying to find her purse.

"Hey, what are you doing?" Was this man robbing her? The man didn't say anything, instead reached down to the floor where her purse had fallen. Megan pulled more frantically at the seat belt that wouldn't unlatch.

"Stop! Somebody help me!" Megan tried to grab her purse strap, to stop the man in any way she could, but he was too strong. And still Megan couldn't make out any of his features.

Once he had what he had come for, the man wasted no more time. He turned and jogged quickly back to the SUV. As soon as the man reached his vehicle, it began to pull away, the damage to it minimal because of the metal bars on the front grille.

Megan watched the vehicle go, trying to get the license plate as blood continued to drip down in her face.

A witness to the accident—some girl who couldn't be more than eighteen years old—ran up to her side of the car and knocked on the window. When Megan couldn't get it to lower, the girl opened the door.

"Oh my gosh, are you all right? I saw the whole thing. That car just plowed right into you, right? Ran a red light and everything. And then just left. That makes it a hit-and-run, right?"

Megan's head was beginning to throb. And still she couldn't get the seat belt to unfasten. Answering the teenager's questions seemed impossible, which was fine because she didn't actually seem to want any answers.

"I've already called the police. That was just so unbelievable. I've got to text my friends and tell them what happened. Oh man, you're bleeding. Are you okay?"

"I hit my head," Megan told her. "And I can't seem to get my seat belt to unfasten."

"Oh my gosh, let me try." The teenager did her best, but couldn't seem to get the belt to budge. "Oh, wait, I hear some sirens."

Moments later a barrage of first responders showed up. A fireman cut the seat belt so Megan could get out of the car and a paramedic helped her over to the ambulance. They offered her a stretcher, but Megan refused.

"You're going to need a few stitches on your scalp. We'll take you to the hospital."

"Fine," Megan told the paramedic. "But first I need to talk to the police. The people who hit me stole my purse and briefcase from my car."

The paramedic called the police officer over and Megan repeated her claim to him.

"Are you saying that because the items just aren't here? Are you sure you had your purse and briefcase in the car with you?"

"Absolutely. Right after the accident, I was sitting right here, and someone walked up, leaned through the window and took my belongings."

The police officer looked skeptical. "You hit your head pretty hard. Are you sure it was someone from the car that hit you that took your stuff?"

Megan's head was really beginning to ache and dealing

with a disbelieving police officer wasn't what she wanted to do.

"I'm telling you, I watched, trapped *right* here—" she gestured to the driver's side of her car "—as a man got out of the passenger-side door of the SUV that had just hit me and walked to my car. I thought he was coming to see if I was okay, but instead he reached into my car through the broken window, grabbed my briefcase and my purse, and then left. He didn't say a word."

The officer shook his head. "I'll put it in my report, but it just seems like a great deal of risk—hitting you with their own vehicle like that—just for a simple robbery. Did you have anything of great value in your purse or briefcase?"

"Less than a hundred dollars in my purse." Then her stomach dropped as she remembered where she had been going and what she had been carrying with her. "Oh no. Ghost Shell and the countermeasure."

"I'm sorry?"

"Stuff for work." Megan shook her head. The countermeasure hard drive had been in her briefcase, as well as all the printouts she was going to use to work from home. The printouts weren't a problem, but the countermeasure? Irreplaceable. This was going to set the Cyberdyne team back. Again. All the way to the beginning.

"Can you provide a description of the man who took your belongings?"

Megan rubbed the middle of her forehead with her fingers. It seemed as though everything in her body hurt. "No, I'm sorry. He wore a hooded sweatshirt that was wrapped tight around his face. And dark sunglasses. I can tell you that he's Caucasian, but that's about it."

"I'll need to get a list of everything that was taken. You'll want that filed for your insurance purposes." Megan could tell the police officer was still skeptical about her story of being robbed.

The medic helped Megan move up onto the gurney so she could be transported to the hospital. Megan felt nauseous and her head was throbbing. She knew she needed to call Sawyer and let him know about the robbery, in case he could possibly do something about it. But she dreaded telling him about losing the countermeasure.

"My phone wasn't in my purse," she told the medic. "Can someone check to see if it's in the car? I need to make some calls."

The medic nodded and went out to talk to the officers. Megan sat against the propped-up gurney. She chewed on her bottom lip, dreading the call to Sawyer. The medic rushed back, placing Megan's phone and lunch bag on her lap.

"Sorry, that's all there was," the woman told Megan.

Megan was placing the lunch bag to the side and picking up the phone when she remembered. She'd been so discombobulated in the break room when Sawyer came in that she had put the countermeasure drive and many of the papers in her lunch bag rather than her briefcase. She double-checked to be sure.

As the ambulance sped to the nearest hospital, Megan laughed out loud. She could tell the medic was concerned about head trauma, but she didn't care.

Megan laughed again. Whoever had just robbed her, hoping to get the Ghost Shell countermeasure, had actually stolen half of a ham-and-cheese sandwich.

SAWYER SCROLLED THROUGH the readout that Cyberdyne's security chief, Ted Cory, had provided. Sawyer's meeting with the man yesterday had been pretty tense. Sawyer pointed out potential security problems, Cory became defensive. Sawyer found that happened a lot when working with civilians. They took everything as a personal criticism.

But Cory had provided all the information concerning

the R & D doors and computer usage without complaint. The problem was that the info was massive. Every time someone accessed a door or a computer, it was logged into the security system. But given the number of R & D employees—even eliminating the ones who had nothing to do with Ghost Shell—the data was considerable.

But what really caught Sawyer's attention was a tiny bit of data that seemed to have been corrupted. It was barely noticeable—if Sawyer hadn't been looking for it, he wouldn't have noticed the discrepancy at all. But a small piece of manipulated data reinforced what Sawyer had been suspecting more and more each day he was at Cyberdyne.

Someone was deliberately sabotaging Megan's attempts to get the countermeasure built.

Certainly bad luck and human error happened, and most of the problems that had belabored Megan and her team could easily be attributed to either. But it was Sawyer's job to look past what could be considered accidental and see the pattern underneath. And now Sawyer was sure it was a pattern.

Sawyer looked at the readout for the vault's security door on the day he had arrived at Cyberdyne. The next morning Megan had discovered the original countermeasure had been damaged while in the vault. Sawyer, of course, had almost immediately accessed the data for who had been in the vault once Megan announced work would resume on the countermeasure. Unfortunately, almost every member of her team had accessed the vault that afternoon or early evening, providing nothing conclusive.

But now, looking at that report for earlier that same day, Sawyer found it: a manual override of the employee code for someone entering the vault the morning Sawyer arrived. Just the smallest of digital fingerprints that had been left behind by someone. No other manual overrides could be found anywhere in the system.

Someone who didn't want their employee ID number to be recognized had gone into the vault the morning Sawyer had arrived. And the very next day the countermeasure had been pronounced damaged beyond repair. It was too big a coincidence for Sawyer to ignore.

Trying to hide their ID number had been a mistake. One someone probably made in a panic when they found out Sawyer was coming and work would resume on the countermeasure. If they had just left the security info alone, it would've never caught Sawyer's attention and clued him in to the fact that someone in Cyberdyne was most likely on DS-13's payroll.

Sawyer pushed back from the computer screen, eyebrows drawing together. A traitor at Cyberdyne could explain many of the setbacks Megan and the team had faced over the past few days. And although Sawyer had no idea who the traitor was, knowing there was someone in their midst changed everything.

Sawyer's phone vibrated in his pocket. Megan. He hadn't expected to hear from her so soon.

Or at all, to be honest, the way she had admitted to not wanting to work around him.

He answered his phone. "Hey, you."

"Hi, Sawyer."

Sawyer could hear people talking and various noises all around her. "Sounds busy. Everything okay?"

"I need you to come pick me up, if you don't mind."

"Uh-oh, car break down?" Sawyer chuckled to himself. Things must be pretty bad if she was calling *him* to come give her a ride.

"Well, not exactly. I was in an accident."

"Are you okay? Where are you?"

Megan's voice dropped in volume a little. "Somebody ran into my car. I'm at the hospital, but—"

"I'll be right there."

Sawyer was already running down the hallway before she could begin her next sentence.

Chapter Seven

Sawyer couldn't quite explain the tightness in his chest from the moment Megan had told him she'd been in an accident, but he couldn't ignore it, either. He'd broken multiple traffic laws on his way to the hospital, pressed by the need to see for himself that Megan was all right.

A flash of his law-enforcement credentials at the ER nursing station got him Megan's room number and silenced the questions about whether he was family and allowed back to see her. There was no way in hell he was going to be waiting out in the foyer.

He found the examination room quickly. She was perched on a table, clutching what looked to be an insulated lunch bag. Her gaze was unfocused across the room.

Sawyer knocked as he pushed his way through the door. Seeing that she was okay with his own eyes helped release the knot in his chest.

"Hey," he said softly, trying to get her attention without startling her.

Her gaze slowly moved toward him as he walked into the room.

"How are you doing?"

"I'm okay. I had to get four stitches in my head." She brought her hand gingerly toward her head. Her voice was soft. "I don't really like needles."

Sawyer walked the rest of the way over to the examination table, not stopping until he stood right in front of her. He was relieved when she didn't move away. "I don't blame you. I don't like them, either. Do you feel up to telling me what happened?"

"I was just driving home—I don't live very far from Cyberdyne. I went through an intersection and a car just came speeding through and rammed into me. Hit me on the passenger side."

Sawyer whistled through his teeth. Depending on the speed and size of the other vehicle, this could've easily been a life-threatening accident. Sawyer was just thankful the vehicle hadn't been coming from the other direction, hitting Megan on the driver's side.

"Was anybody from the other vehicle hurt?"

Megan shifted a little uncomfortably. "Sawyer, after the car hit me, someone got out of it, came up to my car and took my purse and briefcase."

"What?" Shock rolled through Sawyer.

"I was dazed. I'd hit my head on the window and was bleeding. I thought he was coming over to see if I was all right. But he just reached through the broken window and grabbed my stuff."

Sawyer immediately grasped what had happened. This hadn't been a random accident. Someone had deliberately hit Megan's car with the intent to steal from her. And after what he had discovered today at Cyberdyne, Sawyer knew whoever hit Megan wasn't after money. They were after the Ghost Shell countermeasure. Sawyer's curse echoed through the small room.

"You believe me?"

"Why would you make something like that up?" Sawyer turned more fully toward Megan.

She shrugged. "The police thought I might be."

"The police don't have all the facts in this situation."

Before Sawyer could help himself he reached up and touched Megan's cheek. "The most important thing is that you're okay. I'm sure DS-13 were the ones who hit your car and took the countermeasure. I know it's a setback—a big one—but you're still here. That's what matters."

Sawyer didn't tell Megan how lucky she was that she'd been dazed when that DS-13 member approached her car. If she'd tried to fight or keep the man from taking her briefcase, he might've just eliminated her right then and there. It wouldn't be the first time DS-13 had utilized such measures.

But as glad as Sawyer was that Megan was safe, losing what progress had been made on the countermeasure was devastating in a situation where time was already working against them.

"So, do you think you can provide me with a list of everything that was lost? Once I get you home, I'll go back to Cyberdyne and—" Sawyer didn't finish his own statement. What would he do back at Cyberdyne? He had no idea who he could trust.

Sawyer didn't have to finish his sentence anyway because the doctor came in. "Okay, Ms. Fuller, I've signed your release forms and you're free to go." The young doctor looked up from her chart and found Sawyer sitting next to Megan. "Oh, I'm sorry. I'll come back when you're ready."

"No, it's fine, Doctor. You can give any report in front of him."

"Well, you've got no signs of a concussion. That was my biggest concern. You're going to have some pretty big aches and pains for a few days, and your head will probably be very tender from the cut and stitches. But overall it could've been much worse, considering."

The doctor smiled at Megan and then turned and looked at Sawyer. Sawyer gave the pretty doctor his biggest grin, glad to hear Megan was going to be all right. The doctor smiled back.

"Here's a prescription for some pain medication, Megan. Don't be afraid to take it. Call my office if you need anything." She handed the prescription to Megan, and her card to Sawyer. "She probably shouldn't drive today," the doctor said to Sawyer. "Or really do much of anything, just to be sure." The doctor smiled once more at both of them and left.

Sawyer looked down at the doctor's card. Her cell-phone number was written on the back of it. Sawyer was glad Megan would be able to contact the doctor if needed. He reached back to put the card in his pocket when he noticed Megan's odd look.

"Are you okay? Does something hurt? Do you want me to get the doctor to come back?"

"I'm sure you'd be able to do that without any problem."

Of course he would. The doctor couldn't be very far; she'd just left. "Just hang on, I'll go get her."

Megan shook her head. "No, I'm fine. Don't worry about it." It seemed as if cold Dr. Fuller was back rather than the warm Megan he'd been talking to for the past few minutes.

Sawyer rubbed his eyebrows. Okay. "Are you sure?"

"You don't even see it, do you?" Megan asked, still shaking her head.

Sawyer grimaced. Maybe the doctor had been wrong and Megan did have a concussion or something. "See what?"

She seemed about to say something then stopped herself. "Nothing, never mind. You've got the doctor's card in case you want to call her, right?"

"Yeah, she left her cell-phone number on it, too. That was nice. It'll be easier for you to reach her if you happen to need something in the middle of the night."

Megan turned away from him. "Yeah, I'm sure that was her intent."

Wait, did Megan think the doctor had given *Sawyer* her

number? Was that why the temperature had dropped to below freezing in moments flat?

"Do you mind giving me a ride to a rental-car place? My car was completely totaled." Megan was already walking over to the chair where her jacket rested.

"Megan, don't be ridiculous. You heard the doctor. No driving today. I'll take you home. Plus, I need you to tell me everything you remember about the car and man in the accident. Also, a list of everything that was taken."

"That last part is easy."

Sawyer went over to help her put on her jacket, noticing the winces as she moved her arm and shoulder. "Oh yeah? Why is that?" he asked her.

She shrugged then winced again. "The only thing that was stolen was half a ham-and-cheese sandwich."

"What?" Now Sawyer was sure Megan had some sort of head trauma.

She looked up at him with her big brown eyes and smiled. "Um, yeah. I was in such a hurry today in the break room that I put the rest of my lunch in my briefcase and put the countermeasure drive in my lunch bag. The guy today took my briefcase and purse, but didn't even touch my lunch bag. Why would he?"

Sawyer couldn't help it. He reached down and picked Megan up off her feet in a hug, careful not to touch her injured areas. He quickly set her on the ground and watched as her mouth formed a little O. But at least she didn't slap him.

"So you still have everything to do with the countermeasure?" Sawyer didn't release her waist. He couldn't seem to help himself.

"Everything but some papers that are easily replaceable. Yep." Megan reached over and patted the lunch bag she'd set on the examination table. "Right here. I'll bet somebody was pretty pissed off when they saw what was in my briefcase."

Sawyer laughed out loud. He didn't doubt it. He wished he could've been a fly on a DS-13 wall for that discovery.

"Let's get you home so you can rest. No more nonsense talk about renting a car. I'll take you home and drive you wherever else you may need for a while."

"Fine. As long as you promise not to make fun of where I live."

One thing he had to give to Megan, she never said anything he expected her to. "Scout's honor, Dr. Fuller. Lead the way."

Chapter Eight

Walking up to Megan's small house a little while later, Sawyer knew he wouldn't make fun of it; he wondered why she would think he would in the first place. She lived in what he would've expected—a nice neighborhood, with modern amenities and nondescript style. Not much character.

But hey, Sawyer didn't judge. Sawyer's town house outside DC was no prize. Of course, he was hardly ever there. As a matter of fact, there were probably some boxes still unpacked in his closet from when he'd moved in three years ago. Nobody could accuse him of being a homebody. Obviously, Megan was the same.

Sawyer helped Megan from his car and up to the door of her house. She seemed pretty steady on her feet, but his hand hovered at her elbow just in case.

But the inside of her house was the opposite of what Sawyer was expecting. It was the opposite of everything he knew about Dr. Fuller—head R & D computer scientist at a large technology development company.

The interior of her house was as warm and cozy and cluttered as the outside was sterile and modern. Sawyer stopped just inside the doorway, while Megan walked all the way in. She took off her jacket and hung it on what looked like a set of antique hooks attached to the wall. She then walked across the hall into the small kitchen.

"Are you coming in?" she called out as she put a kettle—
a red one with white flowers decorating it—on the stove.

Sawyer slowly took his coat off and hung it on the hook
next to Megan's. He leisurely wandered into the kitchen
looking around.

Megan was watching him. "This is my house," she said,
biting on her lower lip.

Sawyer smiled. "I see that. It wasn't what I was expecting."

"What were you expecting?"

"I guess something closer to what your office looks
like. More—" Sawyer struggled to find the right words
"—organized and contemporary."

"You mean cold?"

Sawyer shrugged. That was what he meant, but it seemed
unkind to say it out loud.

"I know what people think of me at Cyberdyne." Megan's water was boiling, so she turned her back to him to
pour it into two mugs with tea bags. "You probably think
the same thing."

"Not necessarily. I think you have a hard job—made
nearly impossible with all that's going down with Ghost
Shell. You do what you have to do to get the job done. No
fault in that."

She turned and leaned against the counter. "Maybe. I
know I'm not everyone's favorite person. I definitely don't
have a rapport with people like you do."

Sawyer could tell this weighed on her. He walked over
and leaned against the sink so they were closer. "Well, I'm
not able to use the words *symmetric key algorithms* in a coherent sentence like you do. So I guess we're even."

Finally a little smile. He didn't like the way her features
were so pinched. She was probably in a lot of pain from the
accident. "Why don't you go sit down on the couch? I'll

finish the tea and get your pain meds ready. Time to stop thinking about work for a little while."

"But—"

"No buts." Sawyer wrapped his arm gently around her shoulder and urged her away from the counter toward the kitchen door. "You don't need to be Dr. Fuller right now. Just go relax."

Megan tilted her head sideways, looking at him oddly. Sawyer thought for a second she might argue, but instead she made her way into the living room. Good. She needed to just shut down for a little while.

Sawyer finished the tea and got out some of the pain medication she'd had filled at the hospital. He decided to make them something to eat, since he knew Megan had had only half a ham sandwich for lunch—the other half was with some pissed-off DS-13 employee right now. Sawyer's culinary skills were the opposite of legendary, but he was able to warm some soup and find some cheese and crackers for them both. He set it all on a tray he found on the kitchen table.

Megan seemed genuinely surprised when he brought in the food. "Wow, thanks."

She was cuddled deep into the oversize cushions on her couch, a blanket pulled up to her chin. She had kicked off her shoes and her legs were tucked underneath her. Her hair was down from the bun she so often kept it in, brown curls framing her face and shoulders. Her glasses were on the side table.

She barely looked old enough to have her own place, much less be the head computer scientist of anything.

And she was breathtakingly beautiful.

How had he missed that before? Maybe because the past few days he had gotten so used to seeing the prickly Dr. Fuller that he hadn't really noticed the woman underneath.

But here, surrounded by all the things that obviously made her feel at ease, Sawyer couldn't help but be drawn to her.

"My soup-warming skills are legendary, I have to warn you," Sawyer told her as he set down the tray beside her on the couch. "Many a gal has fallen prey to the chicken-noodle wonder."

She giggled. Dr. Fuller actually giggled. Sawyer knew he could easily become addicted to the sound of Megan's relaxed laughter.

"I'll bet. I'll try to control myself." She took a sip of the soup. "Mmm. But it may be hard."

Sawyer sat down on the other side of the couch and began eating his food. Yep, the soup was as bad as he suspected it would be.

"You know, without all your Dr. Fuller gear on—lab coat, glasses, hair pulled back—you don't really look old enough to be head of the R & D department for a company as large as Cyberdyne."

Megan shrugged. "I'm twenty-nine."

Sawyer did some quick math in his head. Her file had told him she had worked at Cyberdyne for eight years, had been head of R & D for five. He also knew she held two doctorates from MIT—but how was any of that possible when she was only twenty-nine years old?

Megan could obviously see his confusion. "Yeah, I went to college when I was fourteen, finished at sixteen. Went on to MIT for my graduate work and finished at twenty."

"Like a master's degree?"

"I got my master's then two PhDs in computer and conceptual engineering."

"While you were still a teenager?"

Megan took another spoonful of her soup. "Well, I was twenty by the time I finished."

Sawyer laughed. "Twenty? That late? What a slacker."

"Actually, one of my dissertation advisers alluded to that."

"That you were a slacker because you didn't finish two doctorates at MIT while you were a teenager?"

Megan shrugged. "Yeah."

"That's absurd."

"No, he was right. I was dragging my feet a little bit my last semester because I wasn't sure what I would do once I was finished with school. I was comfortable there."

"School had to be pretty different for you than for most people."

"Yeah, I was always the little freak."

"C'mon, now. I'm sure that wasn't true." But the way Megan said it, Sawyer knew she felt it was.

Megan reached over and put her empty soup bowl on the large trunk that served as a coffee table. "Nobody really knew what to do with me. I was the scary little kid who could do advanced math problems in her head, but never got any of the pop-culture references and turned a neon shade of pink if anyone used bad language."

"Weren't your parents around?"

"My parents divorced when I was young and I never really saw my dad. My mom remarried a great guy, but they had their own set of kids, twelve years younger than me. My mom couldn't exactly come live with me at MIT with two preschoolers in tow."

She tucked herself back under the blanket. "It wasn't too bad, really. Nobody was ever mean to me or anything. And the intellectual challenge of the doctoral program was exactly what my brain needed."

Sawyer honed in on what she *wasn't* saying. "Yeah, but it sounds like it was pretty lonely."

Megan looked at him with those big brown eyes, her

cheek resting against the soft cushioning of the couch. "It was an excellent opportunity for which I'm very thankful."

Sawyer put his own bowl and plate down and scooted a little closer to her on the couch. He noticed she didn't shift away at all—the total opposite of her actions at Cyberdyne for the past four days.

"It sounds like your college experience and mine are pretty similar," he told her.

That definitely got her attention. "Really?"

"Yeah, except nobody recognized my advanced intellectual giftings, so unfortunately they placed me in a fraternity. It forced me to get average grades and have great parties on the weekend."

Megan laughed. "Yep, sounds exactly the same."

He smiled. "It was definitely an excellent opportunity for which I'm very thankful."

"So how'd you end up going from fraternity to law enforcement?"

He reached over and tucked one of her curls behind her ear. Her eyes began to droop just a little. It had been a long and exhausting day for her.

"That's a long story for another time. Right now, I think we need to get you up to bed. Your body's had quite a shock today with the accident."

Megan shuddered. "I don't even want to think about it. I keep picturing that man with the hood coming toward my car. He was definitely after the countermeasure, Sawyer, I just know it."

Sawyer nodded. "I know you're right. But we'll talk about that tomorrow. Right now you need some sleep. I'm going to stay here and sleep on your couch. Just in case you need anything."

"Oh, okay." Megan stood, but tripped when the blanket she'd wrapped around herself caught her legs. Sawyer caught her just as she was about to stumble face-first onto the ground, a pile of limbs and blanket.

"Careful there."

Megan cringed, heat flooding her face. "Obviously my college awkwardness is not as far behind me as I would like."

Sawyer helped wrap the blanket around her in a more organized, safe-to-walk fashion. "I think anyone who gets T-boned and robbed in one day gets a free pass to be as clumsy as she wants to be."

"I wonder what excuse I'll use tomorrow," she said softly. Sawyer became aware of how close they were to each other.

"We'll just have to figure out tomorrow's problems tomorrow."

She leaned in just the slightest bit closer and Sawyer couldn't help it. He kissed her.

He half expected Megan to turn cold and step back from him unresponsive. But after a moment of surprised hesitation, she let go of her blanket and her arms slid up his chest to his shoulders. And Sawyer found it was him that was caught unprepared. Unprepared for the heat that flared up between them the instant his lips touched hers.

It was fair to say that Sawyer had kissed his share of women, but he couldn't ever remember feeling like this.

His hands slid to Megan's waist. A knot of need twisted in him as he pulled her closer. Had he really ever thought her cold? The very idea was absurd to him now.

Sawyer wasn't sure how long the kiss might have gone on if Megan hadn't made a small sound of pain when Sawyer wrapped his arms around her tighter.

Her head. Her injuries. How could he have forgotten?

Sawyer backed away from Megan just the slightest bit. "We should stop."

He loved the way her eyes opened and blinked up at him half-dazed. "Wh-what?"

Sawyer smiled down at her. "I think we better stop."

"Oh." Megan took a step back. Now her eyes were focused, but Sawyer didn't like what he saw in them. Confusion. Doubt. Embarrassment.

"Just to be clear." Sawyer grasped her waist tighter so she couldn't retreat any farther. "It's not that I want to stop. But you did have an accident today, remember? And you're on some pretty serious painkillers. How about if we try this again soon when those two factors aren't in play?"

Megan gave him a soft smile. "Okay."

THE NEXT MORNING when Megan awoke, she felt as if she had been hit by a truck. Which was pretty close to accurate. She lay in bed, keeping her body still to help with the aches and pains, but her thoughts were flying a million miles an hour.

A lot of them centered on her kiss with Sawyer last night. Megan replayed it in her head with a sigh, feeling like a giddy teenager. Sure, she'd been kissed before— she'd even had a couple of quasi-serious relationships. But those relationships had been with other computer specialists she'd met at different professional functions. The men at these functions, although polite and usually moderately attractive, tended to be relatively boring. Nerds, if she had to sum them up in one word.

They were not, by any stretch of the imagination, as handsome and confident and engaging and *hot* as the man who'd slept on her couch last night.

The man she'd kissed with pretty reckless abandon. And would've kept kissing—and more—if he hadn't stopped them.

Sawyer said he had stopped because he was worried about her injuries. And while Megan appreciated the consideration, she couldn't help but wonder if there was more of a reason why he'd stopped. After all, why would someone who looked like Sawyer Branson—six feet of lean, solid muscle, thick black hair and gorgeous green eyes, who was friendly and confident—be interested in Megan, who was, well, a nerd if she had to sum *herself* up in one word?

Yeah, it was probably good he'd stopped the kiss when he did. They'd both just gotten caught up in a moment. Megan decided she wouldn't bring it up or make a big deal about it. That would just make things awkward and uncomfortable with Sawyer.

Megan sighed. If there was one thing she was good at, it was awkward.

Megan forced herself out of bed, barely holding back a groan. Every muscle in her body hurt. She needed to get some food into her system and take one of the pain pills. Then she needed to get to Cyberdyne. Because besides the kiss with Sawyer, there was one other thing she hadn't been able to stop thinking about. The fact that in order for the SUV that hit her to have known she would be at *that* particular red light at *that* particular time yesterday, somebody at Cyberdyne had to have tipped them off.

There was a traitor working against them at Cyberdyne.

Megan had no idea who it was. She knew she needed to tell Sawyer, although she suspected he had already figured it out.

Megan showered to try to loosen some of the tightness in her muscles, then got dressed and made her way downstairs. Pastries and coffee from the coffeehouse down the street rested at her kitchen table. So did Sawyer, who was reading through the news on his tablet.

"Morning. How are you feeling?" he asked with a smile.

Seriously, could he be any sexier with his deep morning voice? And he brought coffee and food.

"Like I was in a car accident yesterday."

"Ah, yes, an unfortunate by-product of being in a car accident yesterday." Sawyer stood and held out the chair for her at the table. "Why don't you eat something. I'll get your medicine."

"Okay, thanks." Megan sat down as gingerly as she could and began pulling apart a blueberry muffin. "Thanks for staying last night."

Sawyer brought her medicine and a glass of water. "No problem at all. You feeling up to going to work today?"

"That's something I want to talk to you about. I think we've got a mole or a traitor or whatever you want to call it at Cyberdyne."

Sawyer sat back down at the table. "Why do you say that?"

"The people who hit me yesterday. They had to have been waiting for me, knowing when I'd be coming."

"And you think somebody from Cyberdyne tipped them off." It wasn't a question.

"Am I letting my imagination run away with me?" When she said it out loud, it sounded so cloak-and-dagger.

"No. I completely agree with you. As a matter of fact, before I went to pick you up yesterday I found evidence that someone—I couldn't tell who—had tampered with security log-ins for the vault."

Megan pushed her half-eaten muffin away, having no taste for it now. While formulating her theory that someone was a traitor at Cyberdyne, she hadn't considered it would be one of the people she worked closely with. But if someone who had access to the vault was the DS-13 collaborator, then it had to be someone pretty high up in the R & D department. Maybe even someone on her own team.

"What should we do? I can finish the countermeasure myself, but it will take a lot longer."

Sawyer pushed her plate of muffin back toward her. "Maybe not as long as you think, especially if all the problems you've run into over the last few days have really been sabotage attempts. Which would make sense."

Megan ate more of the muffin, running through scenarios in her head. Yes, she could finish the countermeasure herself, but it would mean stepping on quite a few toes. Yeah, there was a traitor, but there were a lot more innocent parties at Cyberdyne who had been working nonstop to get the countermeasure developed. They would not like the idea of being taken off the project.

"We wouldn't be able to tell my team why we're taking them off the project, would we?"

Sawyer shook his head. "No. We need to use this situation to figure out who the mole is at Cyberdyne. We'll have to think of something else to tell your team."

No matter what she told them, they weren't going to like it. Megan finished the last of the muffin.

"This isn't going to get any easier by waiting any longer. Let me go get ready."

Megan got up and was turning to leave the kitchen when Sawyer's arm snaked around her waist. He turned her back toward him gently.

"Because last night's kiss can't possibly be as good as I remember it."

Whatever Megan was about to respond was lost as Sawyer's lips came down on hers. Just like last night, thought of anything but the heat between them flew out of her mind. Megan reached up and wound her arms around Sawyer's neck, feeling him pull her closer with his hands at her waist.

When Sawyer pulled back, they were both out of breath. He rested his forehead against hers. "I guess my memory wasn't faulty at all."

Sawyer put his hands on her shoulders and spun her back around toward the doorway. "You go get ready. Tragically, I have to put saving the world above my own personal wants. But it's not easy."

Chapter Nine

Knowing someone out there was working against them—leaking information, and maybe a lot more, to a group of criminals *intent* on causing harm to innocent people—made just being at Cyberdyne more difficult for Megan. All coworkers, people Megan would've deemed completely trustworthy yesterday, were now cast in the light of suspicion.

Every shut door to an office made Megan wonder if someone was selling secrets behind it. People who smiled and waved seemed fake, those who didn't seemed secretive.

"I don't know how you live in the law-enforcement world," Megan whispered to Sawyer. "I've been doing this for all of thirty seconds and I'm already about to go crazy trying to figure who the bad guy is."

Sawyer chuckled. "Don't overthink it. Just try to act as normal as possible and let them make the mistakes."

Megan snickered. "Have you met me? Overthinking is my middle name."

They entered Megan's office. "Just focus on getting your team off the countermeasure project. Let me worry about looking for suspicious behavior."

Easier said than done. Megan felt a little jumpy just being here. She felt even worse knowing she would upset her entire team by pulling them off the project. Megan took off her jacket, which caused every ache she had from yesterday to announce itself. She winced.

"You okay?" Sawyer came over and helped her put on her lab coat.

"Yeah. Just—" Megan turned to him and smiled wryly. "I'm about to make most of my closest colleagues pretty angry. And I feel like hell. And now the pressure is all on me to get the countermeasure done. And I feel like bad guys are watching me from every corner."

Sawyer winked at her. "But besides that…"

Megan chuckled and walked out of her office, asking Jon Bushman to get the main team together in the conference room. Might as well get this over with.

Trish, the newest member of the team—a talented software developer—was the first to enter the conference room.

"Oh my goodness, Megan!" Trish rushed over and gave Megan a hug. "I am so sorry about your accident. I can't even believe you're back at work so soon. You should've stayed home longer."

The woman was much taller than Megan and her hug pressed right up against Megan's bruises. Megan grimaced in Trish's embrace.

Trish immediately let go. "Did I hurt you? I'm so sorry."

"No, it's fine. Don't worry about it," Megan assured her.

The rest of the team filed in.

"And we heard you were *robbed*." Trish said. "That's just terrible. An accident and a robbery."

How had Trish known that? Megan certainly hadn't told anyone. She glanced over at Sawyer, who shrugged just slightly.

"Where did you hear that, Trish?"

"Oh, honey, are you kidding? Everyone is talking about how they took your purse and briefcase. The audacity of those thieves."

The rest of the team murmured their agreement. Evidently both the accident and the robbery were common knowledge. Everyone provided expressions of sympathy and support, many of them hugging her. Listening to them just made Megan feel worse.

Surely none of these people were the traitor. She'd worked with most of them for years. The thought of it being one of them was devastating to Megan.

"Thanks, everyone, for your concern. I'm feeling much better today." Not true, though it didn't really matter. "But it was pretty scary yesterday."

Megan tried to watch people while she said it, to see if anyone gave away any hint of guilt, but everyone just looked concerned. Megan knew Sawyer was in the corner watching also—maybe he would notice something. She didn't stop to look at him, but his very presence gave her a sense of strength.

"We're going to have to make some changes in what everyone is working on. As of right now, all work on the Ghost Shell countermeasure is to stop."

There were murmurs all around as her team tried to figure out why Megan would pull them off something that had been a top priority just yesterday.

Michael Younker, the oldest member of her team—and often the surliest—was first to speak up. "Megan, what's going on here? First we drop everything for this project, work frantically on it, and now a few days later you're telling us to completely stop." His lips were pinched together.

Megan could understand Michael's frustration. None of the team knew the details about why they had been working so hard on the countermeasure to begin with—the fact that Ghost Shell had been stolen and was about to be sold on the black market. To be jerked back off the project so abruptly was a professional slap in the face, not acceptable for people of the caliber and talent of Megan's team.

"Michael, I understand your frustration." Megan looked

around at her team. "I understand the frustration all of you must feel. But circumstances have changed, and I can't say much more than that. Everyone will need to go back to the projects they were working on last week before we changed focus to the countermeasure."

Michael stood. "Well, I'll be in my office working on older projects until you decide to reroute me on those, too." He stalked out of the room. The other members of the team left also, none of them as upset as Michael, but not happy, either.

Trish stopped to speak with Megan on her way out. "Don't worry about it, Megan. Michael just doesn't do well with abrupt change, you know that. He'll come around." She smiled and then headed out. Megan was preparing to go back to her office when Jonathan stopped her. He had the same pinched look as Michael.

Megan touched Jonathan on the arm. "Jon, I know these changes are a scheduling nightmare for you. Thanks for understanding."

Jon shook his head. "Well, I have to admit, I don't really understand all these abrupt changes. But you're the boss. Do you want me to put the countermeasure project items back into the vault?"

Megan hesitated, unsure of what to tell her assistant. She looked to see if Sawyer was still in the room, but he'd already left.

There was no point trying to hide the fact that she'd still be working on the countermeasure from Jonathan. He had eyes on everything in the lab; it wouldn't take him long to figure it out.

"No. Actually, I'm going to still be doing a little work on it. It's just not going to be a team effort."

"Then I'll help you!" Jonathan perked up quickly. "Two heads are almost always better than one."

Megan knew Jonathan was protective of everything she

worked on. She didn't want to hurt the man's feelings, but neither did she want to invite him in on the project. "I'll let you know if I need help, okay?"

Jonathan didn't say anything else, just nodded and walked away. But Megan could tell she had pricked his pride.

Sawyer caught up to her as she headed to her office. "You doing okay? Doesn't seem to be an angry mob after you."

Megan rolled her eyes. "It looks like I've only totally alienated two of my eight team members, so that's not too bad."

"That Michael Younker guy is no barrel of fun."

"Yeah, he's been like that ever since I arrived. He applied for the position I got. Wasn't too thrilled about it. We aren't ever going to be buddies, but I don't generally have problems with him."

There was a timid tap on Megan's office door.

"Hi, Megan, Sawyer." It was Trish. "Megan, I just wanted to tell you that I don't have many other projects on my plate right now. I know you said we won't be working on the countermeasure anymore as a team, but if you wanted me to work on it individually, I'd be glad to. I just mean I have time to, even if the team is off of it. In case it becomes important again."

Megan looked over at Sawyer, who stood behind Trish. His eyebrow was raised. Megan agreed with Sawyer's skepticism. Why would Trish volunteer for extra work?

"You know what, Trish, I'm not going to have anyone working on the countermeasure right now. But thanks for offering. I know Jon has some new projects that have come in recently. Let him know that you're able to take on a little more. I'm sure he'll appreciate it."

Trish smiled. "Sounds good. And really, I'm glad you're okay from yesterday's accident, Megan." The woman left.

"Her interest in the countermeasure was a little odd, right?" Sawyer asked Megan. "How long have you known her?"

"She's worked here for less than a year. As a matter of fact," Megan said as she looked through a scheduling file on her computer, "she started working here two weeks after I first got in touch with Fred McNeil at the FBI and told him about Ghost Shell."

"That a pretty interesting timeline."

"In her defense, Trish is definitely a go-getter. This isn't the first time she's asked for extra work. She's still trying to prove her value to the team, I think."

"I'm going to do a full work-up on her. On everybody who would've had access to the vault the day I arrived."

"Did you notice anything suspicious while I was talking to the team?"

Sawyer grimaced and shook his head. "No, but that doesn't mean anything. We just keep watching and you keep working."

He was right. Megan was going to have to stop worrying about who the traitor might or might not be and get to work on the countermeasure. That was the most important thing.

SAWYER WATCHED AS for nearly the entire next thirty-six hours Megan labored on the countermeasure. She locked herself in one of the smaller labs and worked constantly, only stopping when he brought her food and to lie down in the early-morning hours.

She was using one version of Ghost Shell—the version he and Cameron had seized from DS-13 a few weeks ago—to create a way to stop the second version still out in the open and dangerous with Fred McNeil. Sawyer didn't even pretend to understand the science behind engineering the countermeasure, but he had no doubt Megan could do it.

She wouldn't let him stay in the room with her, claiming

he ruined her focus. But Sawyer couldn't understand how *anything* could ruin her focus when she was like this. Her concentration was intense—like a professional athlete or a surgeon. Watching her work for the past day and a half, Sawyer had no doubt she was as brilliant as her reputation suggested.

She worked in a room in the line of sight from where Sawyer stayed in her office. He was able to run reports on all of the Cyberdyne employees and still keep an eye on Megan's room. As much as possible he tried to run interference for Megan—the fewer interruptions she had, the quicker the countermeasure would be finished.

The background checks Sawyer ran weren't uncovering anything of much interest or suspicion. It looked as if everyone on the R & D team pretty much lived within their means. No one had made any unusually large deposits or purchases over the past few months.

Trish Wilborne, the programmer who had joined Cyberdyne most recently, was admittedly the most suspicious. But not because of her actions, really just because of the timing of her employment. Sawyer would be keeping a close eye on her. He'd be keeping a close eye on a lot of people. All of whom seemed to be a little miffed that Megan took them off the countermeasure project then proceeded to ignore them all for two days.

They were all gone now; it was late in the evening and everyone had left for the day a few hours ago. It was only Sawyer and Megan. Sawyer enjoyed the quiet and relative darkness of the lab. He was able to not be quite so on guard. He took off his tie and threw it on the table next to his laptop. He stretched his legs out in front of him.

Sawyer was beat. And if he felt this tired, he could only imagine how tired Megan must be with her intense concentration over the past hours. Sawyer didn't know how long they were going to be here. It didn't seem as though

Megan was ever planning to come out of the intellectual cocoon she'd wrapped herself in.

The door to Megan's office burst open. "Okay, that's it. I've got to get out of here." Megan strolled in and began tossing an armful of items and files onto her desk.

Okay, evidently she was planning to come out.

"Everything okay?" Sawyer stood up, bracing himself for another set of technological terms from Megan that he wouldn't really understand about the latest problem with the countermeasure.

But instead, Megan turned and beamed at him. "Everything is fine. Absolutely fine. Hey, where is everybody?"

"Well, since it's nearly nine o'clock, everybody left hours ago."

"Nine o'clock? Wow. I thought it was about noon."

Sawyer shook his head, one eyebrow raised. "You've been in there a long time. I was about to come drag you out for dinner."

"I figured out the biggest part of the problem today, Sawyer." Megan's eyes all but sparkled.

"But I thought you were having trouble." Sawyer leaned on the desk, happy to see Megan so lighthearted. Despite the dark circles under her eyes, she was more relaxed than he'd ever seen her.

"I was. But everything just clicked for me today." She tapped on her temple with her finger. "Sometimes that just happens. It's awesome when it does." She walked unhurried to the door to hang up her lab coat. "Another day or two, Sawyer. That's all I'll need."

With a satisfied sigh Megan perched against the desk next to Sawyer, her shoulder brushing his. "The problem was the block cipher and the substitution-permutation network. Now I can see why we were missing it, since we're coming at it from reverse. We just needed a transposition cipher rather than a Feistel cipher."

Her voice bubbled with excitement, but damned if Sawyer had *any idea* of what she was talking about. If she was anyone else, he'd think she was being smug—using words no mere mortal could possibly understand. But looking at her smiling, upturned face, Sawyer knew she was just sharing her joy.

Sawyer gave a theatrical sigh. "I tried to tell you days ago the problem was the substi-permeated cipher. But nobody would listen."

She actually giggled. "Substitution-permutation network. That's when a network takes a block of the plaintext—"

Sawyer turned and kissed her. A light kiss, just to shut her up and share in her relaxed happiness. But when Megan sighed and melted against him, it turned into something more than light. Sawyer grabbed Megan by the waist and boosted her up onto the desk. A knot of need twisted in him as he grasped her hips and drew her closer. Her lips parted and her arms came up to wrap around his neck.

Sawyer's hands came up to cup Megan's cheeks and entwined into her hair. He tilted her head so he could have better access to her soft warm lips.

But then something made Sawyer tense. In some part of Sawyer's brain that wasn't kissing Megan—the part that had been trained years ago to always be on alert for danger—something registered. Sawyer wasn't quite sure if it was a sound or a motion that had subconsciously grabbed his attention, but something had.

He and Megan weren't alone.

Sawyer pulled his lips back from Megan's and he stepped away from her. Confusion clouded Megan's eyes as she opened them.

"There's somebody else here," Sawyer whispered.

Immediately tension racked Megan's body. "But I thought you said everyone had already left."

"They did. Maybe it's security." Sawyer walked to the office door and called out, "Hello?"

No answer.

Most of the lights throughout the R & D department were still off, casting an eerie shadow among the desks and tables. Sawyer waited a few more moments, then turned back to the office. Maybe his overtired brain was just being too cautious.

But then they both heard it. The clicking of the exit door on the other side of the department. Megan's gaze flew up to Sawyer's.

"Stay here," he told her as he turned and ran out the door.

"Oh heck no," she told him, following right on his heels. They ran to the exit and Sawyer used his security card to open it, looking out into the hallway. No one was there. Sawyer immediately got on his cell phone, calling the Cyberdyne security station.

"This is Agent Branson. I'm in R & D. I need to know the last person who exited the lab."

Sawyer looked at Megan while he waited for the security officer to get the information. Hopefully, this would be a big lead on whoever the mole was here at Cyberdyne.

"Yes, Agent Branson?" The security guard got back on the line. "According to the door security log, Dr. Fuller was the last person to exit the lab besides you."

Sawyer looked over at Megan. She didn't have her security badge around her neck the way she normally did.

"Okay. Thanks for your help." Sawyer hung up with the security guard. He deliberately did not tell the guard about Megan's missing badge.

"It was *my* badge used to open the door?" They began to walk back the way they had come, toward Megan's office. "I took it off earlier this morning when I was trying to catch a few minutes of sleep."

"Where did you leave it?"

"In the room where I was working. But I could've sworn it was there a couple of hours ago."

"You'll have to get a new one tomorrow." Arriving at her office, Sawyer walked in, but noticed Megan had stopped and was looking across the hall.

"What wrong?" he asked her.

"The door to the room I was working in is open," Megan whispered. "I know it was closed before, Sawyer. I *know* it."

Sawyer came out of Megan's office and crossed to the small conference room she had been working in for the past few days. Four different laptops were set up, as well as detailed specs about Ghost Shell and the countermeasure, a soldering iron, and various microprocessors and pieces of hardware. And that was just the stuff Sawyer recognized. It looked like a geek bomb had gone off.

"I don't think anything is missing," Megan told him, looking around more closely. "I brought the countermeasure and all my findings into my office with me a few minutes ago after I finally reached a point where I could break for the day. There wasn't anything valuable here."

"Did you bring your ID badge with you when you left this room?"

He watched as Megan looked around, obviously trying to remember the last place she'd seen her badge.

"No. I remember it was hanging off this chair." She pointed at one near the door. "I wanted to get it, but I had too much stuff in my hands."

That meant—

"Sawyer." Megan figured it out at the same time. "That means someone was in this room while you and I were just down the hall…distracted with each other." Heat flooded her face.

Sawyer half smiled at Megan's reaction and choice of words, but she was right. They had distracted each other and someone had used it to their advantage.

"Are you sure nothing's missing?"

Megan looked around again. "No, like I said, all the critical items I took with me. I was going to put them in the vault before I left. But, Sawyer, whoever came in here—if they were the least bit familiar with the countermeasure—would've been able to see what I've done, the breakthrough I made today."

It was obvious that leaving Megan's work here at Cyberdyne wasn't going to be an option. The traitor was able to get around too easily.

"I'll drive you home." Megan still didn't have a car and there was no way in hell he was going to let her drive herself home alone anyway. "Everything you thought was important enough to bring to your office a few minutes ago needs to go home with you. Cyberdyne isn't safe anymore."

Chapter Ten

A little while later, in Sawyer's car, Megan fought to get all her rushing emotions under control. Elation from making such progress in the countermeasure, adrenaline from the incident in the lab with the spy or whatever, exhaustion from getting only two hours of sleep last night. She wasn't sure which one was taking precedence over the others.

Actually, that wasn't true. She knew exactly what thoughts dominated her head. No matter what thought flooded her mind, her attraction to Sawyer was always at the forefront.

She couldn't stop thinking about Sawyer Branson.

She'd managed to block him out of her mind over the past couple of days as she worked, but it hadn't been easy. She'd done it because it had to be done. And the results had been the much-needed breakthrough in the countermeasure.

But sitting next to Sawyer in this car, she didn't think she'd get him out of her head anytime soon. Not that she really wanted to. As a matter of fact, she'd like to get closer to him. And if the way he'd just grasped her hand was any indication, it seemed as if he'd like to get closer, too.

But he was temporary. Megan couldn't let herself lose sight of that. Sawyer Branson may be interested in her, and they could probably have a wonderful time together, but it would definitely be temporary. When this case was over Sawyer would leave.

Her heart would do well to remember that.

Megan leaned her head back against the headrest and closed her eyes.

"You have to be tired."

Megan nodded. "Yeah. It's been a crazy day."

"I thought we'd go get a bite to eat, but if you're too tired, I can take you straight home."

Before Megan could reply, her stomach grumbled loudly, answering for her. They both laughed. "I guess food is a good idea."

Sawyer pulled over at a local restaurant and they were quickly seated due to the late hour. Megan glanced through the menu—since she was so hungry, everything looked good. She gave her order to the waiter almost at random the first time he came by their table.

The waiter looked at Sawyer. "Just repeat her order for me."

Megan noticed Sawyer's odd look as she handed over her menu. "What?" she asked.

"You." Sawyer half smiled while shaking his head. "You read the entire menu and picked out what you wanted in about eight seconds. I wasn't even through reading the appetizers yet."

Megan shrugged and began to play with a little bit of straw wrapper. "Yeah, I can process information pretty quickly. Do you want to call the waiter back and get the menu again?"

"No. It was just pretty impressive."

"My brain sees information and processes it as a whole sometimes, rather than me having to read individual words. Plus, I was hungry and in a hurry."

"I could tell by the amount of food you ordered. It's nice

to be out with someone who isn't afraid to eat. Although it's hard to believe you can fit that much in your tiny body."

Megan hadn't really thought about how much food she was ordering—but really an appetizer, salad and entrée all for one person was probably a lot. Sawyer was probably used to going out with a different type of woman than Megan. Probably someone much more sophisticated, who actually considered the fact that ordering enough food for a small country might be a little off-putting.

"Yeah, I probably went a little overboard." Megan tried for light laughter, but her laugh sounded uncomfortable even to her.

Sawyer reached over and took her hand from where she was tugging on her bottom lip. "No. Whatever you're thinking in that giant brain of yours…just, no. You knew what you wanted and you got it. Not a thing in the world wrong with that."

Megan gave a wry smile. "And I missed dinner."

"We both did. So thank God for your ability to make a decision and not waste time."

Megan was glad that he really didn't seem to care. She was just so bad at dating. And had no frame of reference at all in going out with someone like Sawyer.

Not that this was really a date. But she had to admit, he hadn't let go of her hand since he took it a minute ago.

"So on your first day you promised to tell me the story of how you ended up here in Swannanoa, even though you didn't really want to be."

Sawyer grinned at her from across the table. He didn't let go of her hand. "Ah, yes, well, I accidentally punched my boss in the jaw and knocked him unconscious."

"How do you *accidentally* punch somebody?"

"I tripped."

"Is that so?"

"Well, let's just say my boss—not the most likable guy

in the world—was sure to say no to an extremely important question my brother was about to ask him. But I'm a clumsy idiot and I fell right into my boss, clocked him in the jaw and basically took my boss out of the equation. Terrible accident."

Megan did not believe for one second that someone with as much masculine grace and control over his own body as Sawyer could have possibly stumbled to such a degree. And she was sure his boss—as soon as he regained consciousness—figured out the same thing.

"So as punishment for your clumsy idiocy you were assigned to us here at Cyberdyne."

"Yeah." Sawyer cleared his throat, looking sheepish. "At the time I thought it was a pretty bad assignment. But I was wrong."

Megan felt his thumb stroking over her knuckles. She looked at their hands—hers was so much smaller than his big, capable ones.

"So your brother works for the FBI, too?"

"Why do you ask that?"

"Just figured he wouldn't be asking your boss an important question unless he also worked with you."

"Yeah, Cameron's in law enforcement, too."

"But not the FBI?"

Sawyer shifted his weight so he was leaning his elbows on the table. He let go of her hand. "Actually, Megan, I can't go into too many details, but no, my siblings don't technically work for the FBI. Really, neither do I."

Megan straightened in her chair. "I don't understand."

The waiter chose that time to bring their food—all of it. Megan had to wait while the plates were set on the table and general pleasantries exchanged before she could get her answer.

"So?" she asked as soon as the waiter was gone. She took a bite of salad while she waited for Sawyer's response.

"Like I said, I can't go into a lot of specific details, but my brother and I work for an interagency task force known as Omega Sector."

"I've never heard of it."

"Well, it's not top secret, but it's also not advertised. The people involved are handpicked."

Megan understood. A best of the best type thing. Megan wasn't surprised Sawyer had been chosen. And since Fred McNeil had been an FBI agent when he stole Ghost Shell, it stood to reason that another agency would be used to clean up the mess he'd left.

"So your brother is part of Omega Sector, too?"

"Yeah, actually, my sister, Juliet is, too. Although she's not an active agent like Cameron and I. At least not anymore."

Megan wanted to ask more about that, but decided not to. She didn't want to put Sawyer in a position of not being able to talk about something. She took more bites of her food.

"So you've got one brother and one sister?"

"And one more brother. He lives in Virginia, runs a charter airplane business."

"Four Branson siblings altogether?"

"Yep, I'm the youngest. And of course, the most charming, best-looking and smartest."

"And don't forget modest."

Sawyer smiled. "That's right. They remind me of that every chance they get."

Megan envied Sawyer his close relationship with his siblings. Megan's brothers were too young for her to be close with, although they were fun little kids.

They ate in companionable silence for a while, both of them starving.

"Any of your siblings married?" Megan asked as she was finishing up her food.

Sawyer shook his head, taking a drink of his water.

"My oldest brother, Dylan, was but…that didn't work out." Megan noticed the slight pause, but didn't push.

"My sister—" Megan could see Sawyer clench his jaw. He cleared his throat and started again. "My sister, Juliet, is…working through some stuff. She's not involved with anybody right now." Obviously whatever stuff his sister was working through was upsetting to Sawyer. Megan reached over and grabbed his hand. She didn't know what to say, but she at least wanted him to know he wasn't alone.

Sawyer ate a few more bites and seemed to collect himself. "Cameron, my middle brother, just got engaged. It's pretty sickening how in love the two of them are." Sawyer gave a dramatic sigh and rolled his eyes. Megan giggled.

They spent the rest of the meal with Sawyer telling stories from his childhood. Growing up with him and his siblings each being less than two years apart meant they had been tight—and had gotten into lots of trouble together. Some stories had Megan laughing so hard it was making her head and side ache all over again.

Sawyer saw her wince. "Come on. Let's get you home." He paid for the food and they headed out to the car.

The drive to her house wasn't long. Sawyer was still entertaining her with stories of childhood antics when they pulled up to her driveway.

"I know you'll be glad to sleep in your own bed tonight rather than the couch at the office. I know I'm looking forward to not sleeping in an office chair."

"First night it was my couch, and last night it was a chair. It hasn't been a great couple of nights for you."

Sawyer winked at her. "Don't you worry about me, sugar. I can handle it."

"Well, I've got a new plan." The words were out of Megan's mouth before she even realized what she was saying. "Why don't you try my bed tonight?"

Chapter Eleven

Sawyer put the car in Park and all but ripped the keys out of the ignition.

Megan's bed was possibly the best plan he had heard in his entire life. Sawyer hadn't wanted to rush things, had recognized that Megan was different from the women he normally dated. She was special. And he was pretty darn sure she didn't take sex casually.

Which, okay, he could admit scared him just a little bit. But heck, everything he felt about Megan scared him. And none of it seemed casual.

Those big brown eyes of hers were looking at him right now, a little in shock at her own words.

"Megan..." There were so many things Sawyer wanted to say. *Yes, please* being the primary one. But he also didn't want her to rush anything. It had been a crazy couple of days. She was tired, had been in an accident, plus what had happened with the unknown intruder in the lab.

Sawyer just wanted Megan to be sure. But couldn't find the right words to say it exactly.

Then Sawyer saw hesitation—the fear of rejection—steal over her face. "It's okay. I understand—" she began softly. She thought he didn't want her.

To hell with that.

Sawyer got out of the car before Megan could finish

her sentence. He strode around it quickly and purposefully, keeping eye contact with Megan through the windshield the entire time. He reached down and opened the passenger-side door.

Megan was still looking at him with those big brown eyes when Sawyer reached down and unlatched her seat belt. He helped her out the door, then promptly picked her up and set her on the hood of the car. He grasped each of her legs just under the knees and slid her all the way to the edge of the hood, hooking her legs on either side of his hips. He stepped forward so they were completely pressed against each other.

"Get one thing straight in that giant brain of yours—I have wanted you from the moment I first thought you were a receptionist and asked you to get me some coffee."

Sawyer grasped either side of her face and tilted her chin up with his thumbs. He brought his lips down very gently to hers, savoring the feel of them.

"And I've wanted you more every day since." He punctuated each word with a brief kiss.

Sawyer slanted her head to the side so he could take advantage of her lips, her closeness. To sink into that soft, wet mouth. He could feel Megan melt against him—both of them wanting to get closer than their current location would allow.

"Let's go inside," Sawyer said to her softly. Both of their breathing was ragged.

Megan nodded. Sawyer reached back inside the car to get the countermeasure items they'd brought home with them—not wanting to leave that out in an unmanned vehicle. Megan got her purse and took out her house keys.

Her eyes were sparkling; no doubt clouded them now. Sawyer reached up and trailed his finger down her cheek. "You're beautiful."

Megan gave a wry grin. "I get lots of compliments, but that's not the usual one."

Sawyer tucked his arm around her as they walked up the stairs to her door. "Oh yeah, what's the usual compliment?"

"Something about my brain. Never about my looks."

"Well, then, you should consider not hanging around with so many visually impaired people."

Megan giggled again—a sound Sawyer was coming to love. Serious Dr. Fuller didn't do enough of it.

Sawyer took her key from her and opened the door, ushering her inside. He closed the door behind them, locking it.

"Saw—Sawyer?"

Sawyer could hear the terror in Megan's voice. He instantly drew his weapon and spun her around so she was behind him.

Her house had been totally ransacked.

Furniture laid overturned and viciously ripped apart, pictures and knickknacks thrown to the ground and broken without care. Someone had definitely searched this place, inflicting the most damage possible while doing so.

If Sawyer had to guess, he would say this was payback for the countermeasure not being in Megan's briefcase when they had attempted to steal it the other day.

Megan whimpered behind him and he wrapped an arm around her, pulling her up to his back, but didn't turn around. Whoever did this could still be in the house.

"Megan, I want you to stay here by the door. I'm going to check things out." When Megan didn't answer right away, Sawyer glanced at her. She was looking around at the ruins of her home, eyes unblinking, obviously in some sort of shock.

Sawyer knew he couldn't comfort her right now. He needed to check the rest of the house, make sure no one was still inside. Sawyer quickly turned all the way around so he could look Megan in the eye, wanting to make sure she understood. "Megan, I'm going upstairs. Somebody could still be here, okay? I want you to stay right by the door. I'll be back in just a second." He handed her the counter-measure drive.

Megan took it, nodding blankly, her eyes still on her destroyed living room. Sawyer wasn't sure she even heard him.

Sawyer walked farther into the living room and kitchen. Both looked clear so he headed up the stairs. Megan's bedroom had not escaped the rampage. Every item of clothing she owned had been dumped out of the drawers and shredded, her pillows, blankets destroyed. He definitely did not want Megan coming up here to see this.

"Just stay down there, okay, honey?"

Sawyer didn't wait for her response. He glanced in the bathroom, then crossed over to the second bedroom Megan used as a home office. This room hadn't been spared, either; papers were spread over the floor and it looked as if part of Megan's computer—the part that wasn't in pieces—might have been taken.

Sawyer was reaching for the closet door when it burst open. Sawyer's weapon was knocked out of his hand as a large man tackled him. Sawyer rolled to the side, but not before he felt the sting of a blade cut into his arm.

The man—in a hoodie, similar to what Megan had described with her car accident—quickly scrambled away from Sawyer and began moving toward the door. Sawyer flipped his leg out, catching the man across the ankles, causing him to stumble, but not fall all the way to the ground.

Both men raced to get to their feet. It was obvious that Hoodie didn't want to stay and fight; he just wanted to get away. Sawyer didn't plan on allowing that to happen.

Ignoring the pain in his arm, Sawyer ran to get his weapon. Hoodie took off in the opposite direction down the stairs. Sawyer was just moments behind him, weapon in hand.

"Stop. You're under arrest," Sawyer called out as the man reached the bottom of the stairs. "Don't force me to use my weapon."

When Sawyer reached the bottom of the stairs, he saw that the man had stopped, but now he was using Megan as a shield. Megan had obviously left her place by the door to come see what the commotion was upstairs and walked right into Hoodie's path. His knife was pointed at her throat.

Sawyer looked Megan in the eyes; she seemed frightened, but not injured. He tried to reassure her with a glance and saw her slide the countermeasure drive into the inside of her jacket. That was his girl—using that giant brain of hers. Hoodie had no idea how close the item he'd been looking for actually was. Sawyer gave his full attention back to the man.

Caucasian. Six feet tall. Close to a hundred and eighty pounds, but light on his feet. Well-balanced.

And a knife at Megan's throat.

The man slowly backed his way toward the door, bringing Megan with him. The perp didn't say anything, but kept himself well hidden behind his human shield. There was no way Sawyer could get off a clean shot.

With each step the hooded man took backward, Sawyer took one forward, weapon still raised and ready to fire. When they reached the front door, Hoodie opened it with one hand, the knife at Megan's throat still in the other.

Sawyer knew the man was going to have to turn and run in just a moment. Sawyer was ready for the chase, knowing he wouldn't be able to use his weapon. He couldn't just shoot a perpetrator in the back as he was running down the sidewalk. This wasn't an action movie. Sawyer had laws he had to obey.

But instead of turning to run, Hoodie took a step forward. The next thing Sawyer knew, Megan was flying toward him—shoved by the assailant with enough force to knock Sawyer down as he attempted to catch her. Hoodie took advantage of their predicament, darting outside.

Sawyer got back on his feet and out the door just in time to see the other man get into his vehicle parked down the street and drive away. Sawyer slammed the side of his fist on the door frame.

"He's gone. There's no way I can catch him now." Sawyer turned back to Megan. She was still on the floor, having scooted so her back was against the wall. Her arms were wrapped around her knees. Sawyer crouched down next to her, running a hand over her hair.

"Are you okay, sweetheart? Did he hurt you?"

Megan unwrapped her arms from her legs and sat up, leaning her head against the wall. "I'm okay. He just scared me out of my mind. I know you said there might be someone still here, but I didn't really think there was. Then I heard the noise upstairs…" Sawyer saw a tear escape one of her eyes.

Sawyer sat all the way down next to her, picked her up and deposited her in his lap. "I'm sorry he got past me. But I'm glad you're okay."

"Does the rest of the house look like it does in here?" Megan gestured to the living room with one hand.

Sawyer hesitated, but there was no point beating around the bush. "Yes. I'm sorry, Megan. It looks like he destroyed pretty much everything."

Sawyer thought Megan might lose it over that news, but she held it together. She wrapped an arm around him and squeezed, then stood up. He knew exactly when she noticed his arm.

"Oh my gosh, you're bleeding, Sawyer. Why didn't you tell me you were hurt? Here I am talking about all my stuff and you're hurt!"

"It's not bad, promise. He came out of the closet cutting at me, but I had on my jacket and shirt, so it's not very deep."

"Do you need stitches?"

"No, definitely not. Maybe just a bandage if you have some upstairs."

"Yes, come up. I'll wrap it for you."

"Megan, you should know, it's not pretty up there."

Megan took a deep breath. "It's just stuff, I know. I keep telling myself it's just stuff. But it's still pretty hard."

"I know it must be." He began walking up the stairs.

"This is tied in to whoever was in the office earlier tonight, isn't it? The one who overheard us talking about the countermeasure breakthrough."

"Without a doubt. The assailant who broke in here obviously thought you'd be here alone with the countermeasure." Sawyer didn't even want to think about that. "You weren't here, so he thought he'd check to make sure you hadn't left it lying around."

They entered Megan's bedroom, where all her clothing lay in shambles. All the color left Megan's face as she realized the extent of the damage. Almost everything she owned had been damaged or destroyed.

"He definitely wasn't subtle about it," Sawyer continued. "And it looks like he just got angrier as he kept searching."

Megan reached down and began to pick up the clothes on the floor, but Sawyer stopped her.

"I know it's hard, but just leave it. I'll have Omega send a local law-enforcement team over here to process this as a crime scene."

Megan dropped the piece of clothing back onto the ground. "My first-aid kit is in the bathroom."

While Megan was getting out the bandage for his arm, Sawyer removed his jacket and shirt, then called Evan

Karcz at Omega. He put the phone on speaker so he could talk while Megan was bandaging his upper arm.

"Evan, it's Sawyer."

"Hey, Sawyer, how's it going with your hot little scientist?"

Megan raised one eyebrow and Sawyer gave her a wry grin. "You mean Dr. Fuller, who is standing right here with me while you're on speaker?"

"Um, yes, well. What I meant was—"

"Save it, Evan." Sawyer could hear the other man's audible sigh of relief in having gotten out of that one. "There's been a break-in at Megan's house."

"DS-13 related?"

"Definitely." Sawyer winced slightly as Megan put some antiseptic on his arm. "It's been totally ransacked. They were looking for the countermeasure. Thankfully, they didn't get their hands on that or the second version of Ghost Shell, or DS-13 would be unstoppable. We had some suspicious activity at Cyberdyne a couple of hours ago, as well." Sawyer explained the incident with the unknown person in the lab.

"So what's the plan?" Evan asked.

"I'm going to have Omega send some locals out here to process Megan's place."

"It sounds like both her work and home have been compromised."

Sawyer shifted so Megan could wrap his arm with a bandage. "When I call in, I'm going to get a local safe house where we can lie low for a few days. But I wanted you to be aware that DS-13 is getting more aggressive. First the car accident, now this."

"There's definite movement in DS-13 with whatever version of Ghost Shell they have. And interestingly enough, whatever is happening is in Old Fort, North Carolina. I'm heading there right now. That's relatively close to you, isn't it?"

Sawyer looked at Megan and she nodded. "Thirty minutes," she told them.

"DS-13 has put word out again that they'll have something to sell—something of great interest—*soon*. A lot of big-name buyers are coming in."

"Including Bob Sinclair?" Sawyer still didn't like this plan of Evan's. There were too many ways Sawyer's sister, Juliet, could get drawn in.

"Yeah, but just Bob. No partner this time." Evan was trying to reassure him, Sawyer knew. "But whatever you guys are doing, Sawyer? Do it soon, man. Things are starting to get hinky out here."

"All right. Be careful, Evan. I guess we both might be out of touch for a while."

"Will do," Evan responded. "You, too."

Sawyer ended the call.

"All right, I patched you up as well as my medical expertise would allow. But I take no responsibility for anything if you get gangrene and your arm falls off." Megan began putting away the first-aid kit, then stopped and just threw it on the counter. "This place is going to have to be burned to the ground anyway."

She turned away and looked back into the bedroom. Sawyer put his shirt back on.

"You can't stay here. Even after the police process it, it's not safe for you to stay here."

"I know." Megan's words were soft, her look lost.

Sawyer reached down and grabbed her hand, twining their fingers together. "We'll make it through this together. But right now we need to get out of here in case our vicious friend decides to come back with friends of his own."

Chapter Twelve

They found a pair of pants and a sweater that hadn't been destroyed and gathered whatever toiletries could be salvaged before heading back to Sawyer's car. Megan took a last look into her house as she was closing the door and about to lock it. What was the point in locking it? If somebody broke in now, they'd probably just run out screaming the way they'd come.

The place she had carved out for herself, her haven, was destroyed. Sure, a lot of it could be replaced: furniture, appliances, clothing. Megan held ample insurance to cover it. But she knew she'd never sit in that house again and feel the same safe, secure level of comfort she had for the past few years.

Megan forced the thought of her house and all her belongings from her mind as she got into Sawyer's car. If she thought about them too much right now, she'd be a basket case. She turned and laid her cheek against the cold glass of the passenger-side window.

"I'm going to take you to my hotel for now. I've got to call all of this in, and you need a few hours' rest."

Megan was too exhausted to argue even if she wanted to. But she didn't want to.

"This is only for a few hours," Sawyer continued. "DS-13 has been putting forth quite a bit of effort to halt the development of the countermeasure. And if what Evan said is accurate, we don't have a lot of time before DS-13 is ready to sell their version of Ghost Shell."

Megan nodded wearily. "I can get started on it again at Cyberdyne first thing tomorrow."

Sawyer shook his head. "I don't think that's going to work. Cyberdyne is too dangerous. Whoever is working for DS-13 on the inside? We don't know who that is or what that person is prepared to do."

Trish Wilborne, the programmer, came to mind at Sawyer's words. Was she the traitor? Time-wise it would make sense. But Megan didn't know if her exhausted brain could be trusted, so she didn't say anything to Sawyer about it.

"I have the critical elements of the countermeasure, but I still need some items from Cyberdyne if I'm going to work on it somewhere else."

"Like what?"

Megan closed her eyes, her face still against the window. "Well, in a perfect world I would need a clean room where I could control environmental pollutants, my electron microscope, a randomizer, EEPROM programmer, a particular digital signal processing chip and programmer, power supplies, capacitors, a breadboard—"

Megan would've continued, but Sawyer reached over and touched her gently on the arm.

"All right, I get it, although I didn't understand half those words. I'll talk to Omega about getting us a safe house where you can work, hopefully some sort of lab, but it probably won't have all of that."

"I could still do it without all of that, but it wouldn't be optimal."

"Well, be thinking about the bare minimum you need, just in case."

Megan nodded, closing her eyes and laying her head back against the headrest. She would think about what items she really needed, but not right now. She was just too tired.

They pulled up at the hotel where Sawyer had been staying when he wasn't sleeping at her office or on her couch. Megan could barely force her muscles to move from the car. She opened the door, but couldn't muster the strength to get out.

Sawyer came around and crouched down next to her open door.

"Hey." His friendly smile was ridiculously sexy. He probably had no idea. Or maybe he did. Megan could only stare at him. "You doing okay?"

"I think I might be broken. I can't seem to get out of the car."

Sawyer reached over and tucked a strand of hair behind her ear and trailed his fingers along her cheek. It was all Megan could do not to lean into his hand. "You've been through quite a lot in the last thirty-six hours. Not much sleep, and then periods of intense adrenaline."

"And a knife at my throat."

"That, too, definitely. It's enough to make anyone's body shut down."

Sawyer stood, reaching into the car to help her out. Megan was glad to find her legs could support her own weight.

"Do I need to carry you?"

"That would be mighty conspicuous, wouldn't it? You carrying me through the lobby and hallway?" Megan giggled.

Sawyer gave her that smile again. "Probably. But no more conspicuous than you keeling over in the middle of the lobby."

"I'll be all right. I'm feeling better."

"You look better." He ran a finger down her cheek. "At least you have a little bit of your color back—you looked pretty traumatized there for a while." Sawyer grabbed the small bag they had packed from her house, slipped his arm around her waist and led them inside and up to his room.

Sawyer only turned on one small light in his room and led Megan directly to one of the beds, pulling the blankets back.

"In you go. You've got to get some rest. We need to go back to Cyberdyne in a few hours for the items you need before anybody shows up there for work."

Megan didn't argue with him, just slipped off her jacket and shoes and lay down in the bed. "What time is it right now?"

"Almost midnight. Get some sleep, sweetheart."

"Don't you need to sleep, too?" The words came out slurred. Now that Megan was lying down, she could barely force herself to stay awake.

"I will. I need to make some phone calls to Omega. But you get the rest you need. I'll be fine."

It was the last thing she heard before sleep claimed her.

SAWYER WATCHED MEGAN fall asleep right in the middle of their conversation. That was fine; her body and mind were obviously exhausted. Sawyer tucked the sheet and comforter around her more securely. He wished he could erase that traumatized look she'd had at her house. How the hell were things snowballing out of control so fast?

Sawyer moved to the table on the opposite side of the room so he was less likely to disturb Megan, although he doubted anything would wake her up right now. He dialed in to Omega, wishing his sister, Juliet, was at the office. She worked an odd mixture of desk jobs at Omega—part analyst, part handler. She was too good to really be either, but that was what she wanted right now, and Sawyer and his brothers supported her.

But it was midnight, so Juliet probably wouldn't be in

the office when Sawyer called in requesting the special-
ized safe house he and Megan needed so she could get the
countermeasure work finished. He'd just be talking to a
random handler. Not how Sawyer preferred it, but right
now his only option.

Sawyer made the call, first providing his credential and
identification codes. He then gave the handler the information about the break-in at Megan's home and their need
for a specific type of safe house. Sawyer felt better after
the call was completed. Although Sawyer didn't know the
handler personally, he seemed competent and ready to find
Sawyer what he needed. Sawyer knew local law enforcement would be called out to Megan's house and the scene
processed. If anything of any value showed up, Sawyer
would be notified immediately.

Knowing that was taken care of, Sawyer felt more relaxed. It was now nearly one o'clock in the morning. Sawyer
knew he needed sleep himself. Sawyer looked at Megan's
sleeping form in the bed. She had held up so well over the
past couple of days, but he was afraid things were only
going to get more difficult. If what Evan said was true and
DS-13 was really close to having their version of Ghost
Shell ready, he and Megan had to work even more quickly
than Sawyer had originally thought.

DS-13 calling buyers to an area so close to them here
in Asheville really caught Sawyer's attention in the same
way it had caught Evan's. Had DS-13 gotten someone from
Cyberdyne to help them finish their Ghost Shell? Was it
the same person who had been sabotaging the countermeasure work?

That would make a lot of sense.

Sawyer knew Megan had a hard time thinking of one
of her team in the R & D department being the culprit, but
it had to be. He and Megan needed to get to Cyberdyne,
retrieve the necessary items and get out before that per-

son came in to work tomorrow. Sawyer would then take Megan to a secure location so she could finish her countermeasure magic.

Sawyer kicked off his shoes and lay down in the bed next to Megan. The thought of sleeping in the other bed—even for the few short hours they had—wasn't even an option. In his mind, Sawyer kept seeing that knife pointed at Megan's throat. It was a picture he'd take with him to the grave.

Megan was lying on her side, facing away from him. Sawyer slid one arm under her shoulder, wrapping it around her, hooked his other arm around her hips and slid her back against him. Megan murmured sleepily for just a moment, then relaxed in his embrace.

As tired as he was, Sawyer wanted to enjoy a few moments of just holding her. It was an unusual feeling for Sawyer—he didn't tend to be a cuddling type of guy. But something about Megan brought out his protective instincts. Maybe it was her savvy brilliance layered with shy beauty. An odd mixture, unique to Megan.

Megan was unique and appealing to Sawyer in ways he never thought possible.

Sawyer pushed those thoughts out of his mind. He was here to protect her and to do whatever needed to be done to get the countermeasure complete. And although she was an itch he definitely hoped to scratch at some point, there was no need to get caught up with flowery emotions.

He liked her. He was sexually attracted to her and was sure she was attracted to him, too. But she was the job. He'd do well not to forget that.

Sawyer fell asleep pulling *the job* closer to him.

MEGAN AWOKE TO Sawyer gently squeezing her shoulder. He was standing right beside her, freshly showered and ready to go.

"Good morning." He smiled at her, but it wasn't the same

relaxed grin he'd had last night. "I know you must still be tired, but we need to get to Cyberdyne before anyone else arrives there."

Megan sat up. "What time is it?"

"Almost 4:30. You need more rest, I know, but like I said—"

"No, it's okay." Megan swung her legs over the side of the bed. "Just let me take a quick shower and we can be on our way."

"Sure." Sawyer had already sat down, typing something into his phone, not really paying her much attention.

Megan wasn't sure what she had expected—a good-morning kiss? More of his sexy smiles? She couldn't put her finger on what the problem was, but it seemed as if last night's quiet intimacy—at the restaurant, before the traumatic break-in and even afterward when they'd arrived here at the hotel—was now gone.

But Megan could've sworn in the middle of the night, when she'd barely woken up for just a moment, that she'd been lying in Sawyer's arms. Maybe her unconscious mind had imagined it just to soothe her.

Megan glanced over at Sawyer again. He was still messing with his phone. Megan began to speak to him, but then decided to leave it alone. She walked to the shower instead.

The shower helped her feel better, washing away some of the feeling of violation that had come from seeing everything she owned in shambles. The hot water and few hours' sleep fortified her; she felt stronger, not so overwhelmed. Ready to get the countermeasure finished.

And Sawyer had a lot on his mind. There was no reason to assume he was creating distance between the two of them on purpose. He was stressed trying to figure out who the traitor was at Cyberdyne, keep Megan safe, get ahead of DS-13. It was a lot. And she'd only talked to him for two minutes, and not her most alert two minutes at that. No need to borrow trouble.

Megan changed into her recovered outfit and put on what makeup she had. She quickly braided her hair so that it fell neatly down her back.

Coming out of the bathroom, Megan heard Sawyer on the phone. Whoever he was talking to, Sawyer wasn't happy with the conversation.

"We knew there was a probable security breach, Mr. Cory. That's why I was sent here in the first place."

Ah, he was talking to Cyberdyne's head of security, Ted Cory. Sawyer gave Megan a curt nod of acknowledgment.

"Dr. Fuller needs to finish the project she's working on. I'm not exaggerating when I say it's of national-security importance that she finish it."

More talk from the other side. Sawyer stood up in disgust.

"We've already established that the Cyberdyne labs have been compromised, Cory. She can't work there safely. The Cyberdyne board of directors isn't taking into account—"

Megan watched as Sawyer's grip on the phone became white-knuckled.

"No, the FBI doesn't have a subpoena for the equipment. So, yes, it is still Cyberdyne's property." Sawyer shook his head. "Then I guess she'll have to work on it at the lab. But I want it on record that I don't think this is the best solution. Dr. Fuller is sleeping right now, so tell the lab not to expect her until midday. She'll bring the countermeasure with her when she comes in."

Sawyer listened, rubbing his eyes.

"When are you meeting with the security team to let them know? Fine. If it's okay, I'll sit in on the meeting in case I can be of any assistance to you or answer any questions."

Sawyer disconnected the call and all but threw his phone down on the table in disgust.

"So, that didn't sound very promising."

"I called the head of security to bring him up to speed. I was about to let him know your badge had been stolen and that we were coming in to get the equipment you need in just a few minutes. Then he informed me that Cyberdyne is basically on lockdown in terms of equipment."

"What? They've never done anything like that. I've always been able to take work home with me as long as I clear it through the right channels."

"Evidently there was a meeting with the president and board of directors sometime yesterday with concerns about what is happening security-wise. Nothing—equipment, technology—is supposed to leave Cyberdyne. You're required to return Ghost Shell and the countermeasure immediately. Cory's holding a meeting to notify the entire security team of the new policy at seven o'clock."

"So I'll have to work at Cyberdyne." Megan didn't like the idea, but didn't see any way around it.

For the first time Sawyer really looked at her. The hardness in his eyes softened and he crossed the room to sit next to her at the foot of the bed. "Megan, if you do that, we'll be playing directly into DS-13's hands. They want us trapped there at Cyberdyne, where you're always being watched and they can keep trying to do damage."

"You believe DS-13 is behind the lockdown at Cyberdyne? Do you think Cory is in on it?"

"DS-13 behind the lockdown wouldn't surprise me. Omega recently found out that DS-13 is more far-reaching and powerful than we thought. But I doubt Cory is actually working for them. The pressure on the chief of security for the lockdown at Cyberdyne is coming from the board of directors. It would've been very easy for DS-13 to just put a bug in the ear of one of the board members about security. Then sit back and watch it domino. Cory is just a pawn."

Megan took a deep breath and blew it out, shrugging.

"Regardless of who put pressure on whom or why, the outcome is still the same. They're not going to let us take anything out."

"That's right. Once Cory has the meeting at seven o'clock with the security team, nothing's getting out. Furthermore, they're expecting you to be in around noon and to turn over all Cyberdyne property you have in your possession."

Sawyer was looking at her intensely. The way he emphasized his words were odd. Then it clicked for Megan—Sawyer wasn't telling her these details because he had accepted them as their circumstances. He was telling her so she also could see the tiny hole they were about to try to fit through.

"But I'm not going to be there at noon, am I?" Megan asked him. "We're still going right now to get everything out before security learns about the new policy."

Sawyer nodded and took her hand. "That was my thinking. But you have to be sure, Megan. You and I know how important the countermeasure is, but Cyberdyne probably is not going to see it that way—at least not for a while, if ever."

Megan looked down to where Sawyer had linked his hand with hers. Gone was the coldness and distance she had felt between them earlier. "I know," she whispered.

"Omega will do its best to explain to Cyberdyne why you did this, and why it was important and necessary, but it won't make a difference for a while. You'll basically be cut off from Cyberdyne."

Megan didn't want to waste any more precious time arguing about this. Losing her job was nothing compared to the cost of a terrorist group having access to the damaging capacities of Ghost Shell with nothing in place to stop the damage. It would basically turn the government's own communication equipment against itself—crippling law-enforcement agencies and first responders. It would leave the country wide-open and vulnerable for an attack.

Thinking about it that way, Megan didn't even have a choice. She had to get the countermeasure completed and in place as soon as possible. No matter what it cost her.

Megan stood. "Let's go. We don't have any time to waste if we want to get in and out before the security briefing."

Sawyer stood up and drew her into his arms for a tight hug. Megan leaned in to him, trying to draw some of his strength. "You're amazing," he whispered. They pulled apart, gathered their stuff and headed out the door.

Megan couldn't help but think she'd already lost her car and her home in an attempt to complete this project. Plus now it looked as though she was about to lose her job.

Megan glanced at Sawyer walking beside her in the hallway. He reached over and put an arm around her, pulling her to his side as they walked. He looked down at her—warm, sexy smile back in place.

Megan just hoped by the time it was all over she wouldn't also lose her heart.

Chapter Thirteen

When Sawyer had awakened that morning—his internal clock making an alarm unnecessary—Megan had still been wrapped in his arms. Except to turn to face each other, he didn't think either of them moved from the embrace the entire time they had slept. Staring into her face—her features so relaxed and young-looking in sleep—Sawyer knew the best thing he could do was put some distance between them. Before things became any more complicated than they already were.

He could tell that Megan picked up on it right away. Her giant brain had been working at full capacity from the moment she opened those brown eyes. She hadn't said anything, but he'd recognized the slight confusion over his withdrawal.

Of course, that decision to withdraw had been shot to hell when Sawyer saw—once again—Megan's strength and determination. Her willingness to sacrifice her job, although hopefully it wouldn't come down to that in the long run, and do what had to be done with the countermeasure spoke volumes about her. Sawyer found he wasn't able, and sure as hell wasn't willing, to try to keep the distance between them when she was willing to put so much of herself on the line.

He'd just have to deal with the tomorrows as they came.

Right now, he wanted to keep Megan as close as possible. He glanced over at her in the passenger side of the car to make sure she was okay. Her eyes were worried, but she gave him one of her shy smiles.

Sawyer had been smiled at by many women over the years, but none of them took his breath away the way Megan did.

Sawyer's phone buzzed, catching his attention. It was Omega, with a secure code, letting Sawyer know they had received his update about the circumstances at Cyberdyne changing and his plan to remove the equipment needed to finish the countermeasure. An appropriate safe-house address would be delivered soon.

That was the great thing about working for an elite task force like Omega: the ends justifying the means was regular practice. Bending some rules when necessary, such as removing needed items from a company, even though said company had forbidden it, wasn't even frowned upon in Omega. Omega always kept the big picture as the priority. And the big picture now was getting that countermeasure finished.

Sawyer was glad they would have the safe house ready soon—once he and Megan left Cyberdyne with the stolen equipment, there would be no coming back. They were pulling through the outer gate of Cyberdyne security now. Sawyer showed the guard both his temporary Cyberdyne badge and his law-enforcement credentials and the guard waved them through.

Sawyer relaxed just the slightest bit. The guard hadn't asked to see Megan's security badge, nor had he seemed to recognize who she was, so obviously the security team wasn't on high alert yet. Which was good, because Megan didn't have a badge to show him.

Sawyer parked the car in the closest spot to the front door, not difficult since the lot was nearly empty. He backed the car in so it faced forward out of the parking spot. It might save them precious seconds if they were leaving in a hurry. But Sawyer hoped it wouldn't come down to that.

Sawyer turned to look at Megan. "All right, sweetheart, are you ready? Remember, we can't take the flux capacitor and everything else you listed last night." Megan's eyes narrowed at the '80s movie reference, but he didn't stop to explain it to her. "Only the most essential items. And only what we can carry out in a backpack, very low-key."

Megan nodded. "I know what I need. But I should warn you, if I get bored and want to build a DeLorean time-travel machine, that's going to be difficult without a flux capacitor."

Sawyer reached over and kissed her. He couldn't help it. "Then by all means, grab the first flux capacitor you see."

They got out of the car, the brisk winter air surrounding them, the sun having not even risen yet. "Okay, just try to act as natural and relaxed as possible. There should only be security guards around at this time. Just talk to those you normally would, and keep it as brief as possible." Sawyer ushered her in the door. They needed to get a move on; it was already nearly 6:00 a.m.

Sawyer used his badge, which almost had the same clearance as hers anyway, to get them in the main Cyberdyne doors. The overnight guard working the front desk seemed a little surprised to see anyone coming through the door at this hour, but not suspicious. Sawyer saw the guard slide a magazine of dubious type to the side and under some papers.

Good, let the guard be more worried about getting caught looking through his dirty magazines while on the job than wondering why he and Megan were here at such an early hour. Or worse, wanting to see Megan's badge.

"I've met a lot of the security team, but not you. I'm

Agent Branson. Dr. Fuller and I are getting an early start on the day."

The man swallowed hard. He knew he'd been caught doing something worth reprimand. "Uh, yes, sir."

Before the man could flounder any more, Sawyer cut him off. "I understand you have a full security team briefing at 0700? I'll be there for that." The man nodded. "Until then, I trust that this front door is being watched more by security than it was when I entered?" The man nodded again, wide-eyed.

"Um, yes, sir. Sorry, sir."

Sawyer just turned and led Megan down the hall.

"Wow, pretty impressive, Agent Branson," Megan said once they were out of earshot. "I didn't think you had that in you."

Sawyer winked at her. "Well, sometimes boyishly charming is not the way you want to go. Now that guy will be worried that I'm going to bring up at the security meeting the reading of certain types of magazines at the front desk while on duty. He won't be thinking about what we're doing at all."

"Who has a giant brain now?" Megan asked him.

Sawyer smiled and used his badge to let them into the R & D lab. "Okay, get what you need and let's get out. Is there anything I can help you find?"

"No, I know what I need and where to find it, but it will take a while. Some of it has to be separated from the main system and programmed to be available for use elsewhere. That means I'll need to…" Megan was already walking toward what she needed as she spoke, her voice trailing off.

Sawyer kept an eye on the door as Megan moved frantically around the lab. Every once in a while he could hear her talking, but knew she wasn't speaking to him. She was having arguments with herself, so he left her alone.

Sawyer logged in to the security system so he could see who was coming into the building. A few early birds, mostly sales or office managers had logged in, but no one from R & D yet, thankfully.

"How's it going?" Sawyer called out.

"I'm almost done. Five minutes. I just need to bypass this system." Sawyer could hear her fingers clicking on the keyboard.

Five minutes was okay. That should give them enough time to get out before Ted Cory got there for the seven-o'clock meeting. If he saw Megan here, after Sawyer told him she wouldn't be in until midday, they were sunk.

But then the screen flashed an ID badge Sawyer was definitely not expecting.

Megan's. Damn.

Whoever had stolen Megan's badge yesterday was back. Even worse, this meant as soon as Cory arrived, he would be alerted that Megan was in the building.

Sawyer watched the screen as Megan's assistant, Jon Bushman, and Trish Wilborne also logged in through the front door at the same time. They were obviously coming in together. Megan's theory of Trish being the mole was looking more conceivable.

Things were going to hell quickly.

"Megan, time to go," Sawyer called out. "Right now. We've got all sorts of problems."

Megan rushed over to the desk with the backpack full of the items she needed. "Okay, I've got it all. What's going on?"

"Well, *you* just logged through the main door."

"The person who stole my ID badge?"

"Yep." Sawyer cursed under his breath when he saw the next entry in the front door. Ted Cory, head of Cyber-dyne security.

"All right, we've got to get out of here. Everybody and their brother has decided to show up early."

"Who?"

"Both Jon Bushman and Trish Wilborne showed up together, not long after your badge was swiped through the door."

"Trish Wilborne? I really think she's the mole, Sawyer. It makes more sense than anybody else."

"I'm beginning to agree with you. But we've got another problem now, too. Ted Cory just logged in. Damn it, we've got to get out of here."

Megan handed Sawyer the bag full of equipment. "Here, you take the stuff and go. Get it out of the building. That's the most important thing. I'll say my hellos, act like everything is normal and get out as soon as I can."

Sawyer didn't like the thought of splitting up, but didn't see any way around it. Jon and Trish were going to be here any moment. And Ted Cory would check the log first thing and find out Megan was in the building. Once he did that, neither she nor Sawyer would be able to leave with any items.

But Sawyer was afraid Cory might not let Megan leave at all.

"Okay, we'll split up. I'm going directly to the car. You get out of here as soon as you can behind me. Don't let Ted Cory corner you. You won't have a bag, so that's not quite so suspicious, but he can demand that you return Ghost Shell and the countermeasure, and if you don't he could have you arrested."

Megan nodded.

"Don't let anybody get you alone. We don't know who we can trust, so we can't trust anyone," Sawyer continued. Megan nodded again. Sawyer could hear Jonathan and Trish talking as they entered in the door to the R & D lab.

Sawyer bent down and kissed Megan hard, briefly. "I'm going to stay out of sight until I can get past those two. Hurry," he told her and strode out one of the side doors, so no one could see him. He didn't like this at all, but he didn't see any other choice.

MEGAN WATCHED SAWYER disappear around the corner just as Jon and Trish walked in. Megan clutched her hands in front of her. What was she going to say to them?

Just act normal.

That probably included not jumping on Trish and punching the other woman until she admitted she was the traitor. And it was barely six o'clock in the morning. What were they doing here so early?

And why were they here together at this hour? The pair hadn't noticed Megan yet and she watched as Trish brushed up against Jonathan and he smiled down at her.

How long had this been going on? Had Trish seduced Jonathan? Was she trying to get close to him to get information? Or maybe access to something he had that she didn't? It would make sense. Jonathan looked completely enamored with Trish.

How had Megan never noticed this before? Jonathan was always so tense and uptight around the office. Megan had never actually thought about his personal life outside Cyberdyne.

But evidently he had one. And evidently Trish was part of it. For how long Megan didn't know.

Megan was supposed to act normal around them. But what was normal? Normal for not suspecting one of them was a lying traitor was different than the normal reaction for the boss finding out two underlings were sleeping together.

Both of which were a different normal from having to get the hell out of there as quickly as possible to avoid arrest.

"Oh my gosh, Megan!" Trish finally noticed her. Trish

and Jonathan all but leaped apart. "What are you doing here so early?"

Megan had to hand it to Trish, she didn't look panicked at seeing Megan here at Cyberdyne, just embarrassed at being caught in an illicit situation. "Maybe I should be asking you guys the same thing," she told them, one eyebrow raised.

Trish and Jonathan looked at each other briefly, then back at Megan.

"Actually," Jonathan spoke up, not quite meeting Megan's eyes, "we thought we would get here early and get our work out of the way, then try to talk you into letting us help with the countermeasure when you got in. But you're already here."

Megan wanted to stay and ask more questions—see if she could get any information out of Trish in particular—but knew she needed to get going. Once Ted Cory knew she was in the building, getting out would be much more difficult.

Plus, it wouldn't take Trish or Jonathan long to figure out items were missing if they got back in the lab and started looking around.

"Actually, I've been here all night." Megan ran a hand over her face in mock exhaustion, hoping they wouldn't notice she was in different clothes. She decided not to bring up the obvious relationship between Trish and Jonathan. She didn't have time, and compared to everything else that was going on, it really didn't matter. "I'm about to go get some breakfast at the cafeteria and head outside for a few minutes to get some air."

Megan began walking to the door, but realized she didn't have her badge. The badge was needed to get in or out of the R & D lab.

"Hey, Jon, do you mind scanning the door for me? I left my badge in my office. I just want to grab something to eat super quick." Megan spoke to Jonathan, but looked right at Trish, searching for any changes in her expression that might give the other woman away. But there was nothing. As a matter of fact, Trish was just staring at Jonathan, looking gooey.

But the question seemed to catch Jonathan off guard. "Um, what? Well, sure, that's no problem, I guess." He walked over, scanned his badge and opened the door.

"Okay, thanks. I'll see you guys in a few minutes."

"Should we get started on anything?" Trish called out to Megan just as she was turning away. "I know you said you didn't want anybody else working on the countermeasure, but Jon and I were talking about it and we really think we could help."

Yeah, Megan just bet Trish thought she could help. Jonathan shot an irritated look at Trish, then smiled sheepishly at Megan. "Whatever, boss. Just wanted you to know we were ready to help if you need it."

Megan glanced down the hallway; the way she needed to go was all clear. But when she looked the other way, a door was opening. Ted Cory stepped out into Megan's line of sight.

She needed to leave. Right now.

"Thanks, Jon. We'll talk about it when I get back from breakfast, okay? I'm famished."

Jon was about to respond, but Megan turned and began walking down the hallway.

"Megan, how are you going to get back in the lab without your badge?" Jon walked out after her.

Megan turned, but kept taking steps in the direction of the exit. "I'll just have security let me in. No problem." She could see Ted Cory making his way toward them. He would see her any second.

"Well, just hang on, I'll run and get the badge for you, so you can have it."

Megan did her best to keep Jonathan between her and the director of security so he wouldn't be able to see her, but that wouldn't work for long. She stopped her backward walk so she could get rid of Jonathan. She didn't want him trying to come with her all the way to the cafeteria, where he thought she was going.

"That would be great, Jon. Thanks so much."

Jonathan nodded and turned back toward the R & D lab. As soon as his back was to her, Megan began walking briskly down the hall. She glanced over her shoulder and saw Ted Cory talking to Jonathan. Evidently he asked Jonathan where Megan was, because Jon was pointing right at her. Ted turned and began moving in her direction.

Megan walked as fast as she could without outright running. She didn't want anyone to put the building on lockdown because of suspicious behavior on her part. Then she'd never get out. Megan wasn't far from the main doors.

She didn't know why Ted Cory wasn't calling after her. Maybe Jonathan had told him she was going to the cafeteria and he planned to follow her there to talk to her.

Megan made it to the main foyer. If she turned to the left she would only have a little bit to go to get to the main doors, but knew she wouldn't have enough time to make it to them if Cory radioed for the locks to be set. So instead she turned to the right as if she was going to the cafeteria.

Halfway down that much shorter hall she looked over her shoulder. It looked as if Ted Cory wasn't following her anymore, or if he was he had paused for a moment. Megan ducked inside the women's bathroom.

Megan waited, ear pressed against the door, hoping to hear the security chief pass her. She prayed he would think she had gone the few more yards to the cafeteria. Although all he really had to do was stay at the security desk near the front door. She wouldn't be able to get past him.

After just a few moments she could hear someone talking as they went down the hallway. It was definitely Ted Cory, sounding as though he was talking to another one of the guards.

"I want you to keep an eye on her while we have the all-hands meeting. She is not to leave this building under any circumstances until I have a chance to interrogate her."

Megan didn't like the sound of the word *interrogate*.

Their voices became softer as they passed by the restroom door and continued toward the cafeteria. As silently as she could, Megan opened the door and began walking back toward the main door, praying Cory hadn't said anything to whoever was working the front desk.

She forced herself not to look back as she quickly covered the ground to the main door. She smiled at the security guard at the desk—he smiled back, so evidently Cory hadn't talked to him about her yet—and continued casually toward the door.

"Going outside?" the guard asked.

"Yeah, just need some fresh air." Megan smiled again, but kept walking.

Damn. Megan realized she didn't have her badge. She couldn't get through the door at this hour without it and definitely didn't want to ask the security guard to help.

Megan pretended to crouch down and tie her shoe while she got out her phone and sent a text to Sawyer to meet her at the door. She knew the car wasn't very far; he could be here in just a few moments if she could just stall.

Megan tied the other shoe while she was down there and pretended to dust something off her foot. There, that should be enough time for Sawyer to be at the door once she crossed the lobby. Megan stood, ready to move.

She was startled by a hand grasping her shoulder and spinning her around. Ted Cory stood glaring at her.

"I got a message earlier that you would be here this morning earlier than I had been told. Going somewhere, Dr. Fuller?"

Chapter Fourteen

Megan kept her expression neutral and her posture relaxed as she faced the director of security, hardly listening to what he was saying. She thought fast.

"Hi, Mr. Cory. Just thought I'd step outside for a few moments to get a little fresh air. It's been a long couple of days—I've put in a bunch of hours. I'm feeling pretty stiff."

As if to demonstrate, Megan reached her arms over her head and linked her hands, stretching her back and torso. She glanced over and saw Sawyer walking up to the glass Cyberdyne doors. Megan shifted to the side so Mr. Cory would be less likely to see Sawyer's approach.

She was going to have to make a run for it. Megan hoped Sawyer would be ready. Once she began running, he would only have a few short moments to get the door open before a member of security remotely overrode the locks. The chances of Megan getting out were slim. At best.

"You don't have any items belonging to Cyberdyne on your person, do you, Dr. Fuller? You may or may not have heard, but due to recent security issues we are initiating a mandatory lockdown policy. No items are to be taken from the building."

Megan patted down her thin sweater. "Nothing on me, Mr. Cory. And I think the lockdown is an excellent idea. It's important for Cyberdyne items to be safe."

Mr. Cory still looked at her sternly, standing between her and the door.

"The policy also means you'll need to return any items you've taken out of Cyberdyne. Even if it was acceptable in the past for you to remove them, it no longer is."

"Absolutely." Megan nodded enthusiastically. "I brought everything in with me this morning. They're all in the R & D vault. Would you like to come down with me and see?"

Cory relaxed minutely. Obviously he felt if Megan was willing to escort him to the R & D vault she really had returned the items she'd taken yesterday. Either that or Cory knew he'd have Megan in his office for interrogation if she hadn't. Either way, Cory felt he had Megan where he wanted her.

This was Megan's best chance to escape, while Cory was slightly more relaxed. "Dang it, this shoe just won't stay tied." While bending down to tie her shoe again, Megan glanced out the door. Sawyer was there. Ready.

Megan threw herself upright, grasping her arm with the other hand and jabbing her elbow as forcefully as she could into Ted Cory's stomach.

Not expecting the blow, the man doubled over. Megan began running for the door as fast as she could. Behind her just moments later she could hear the commotion as the other security guards struggled to figure out what was going on.

Megan saw Sawyer use his badge to open the sliding doors. They slid all the way open, but almost immediately began closing again. One of the guards was manually overriding the door.

Megan ran faster. There were only a few yards to go, but she wasn't going to make it.

Then Sawyer moved forward and wedged himself in the closing door, his back against one edge, foot and hands against the other. Megan knew he wouldn't be able to hold it for long, and once it shut she wouldn't be able to get out.

"C'mon, baby, you can make it," Sawyer called to her, teeth gritted, body straining.

In a final burst of speed, Megan scampered through the door opening, under Sawyer's leg where he was holding it with all his strength. As soon as she was through, Sawyer dived out of the door and it slid shut. Sawyer helped Megan up from the concrete and they ran to the car.

The closed door now worked in their favor as the security guards were locked inside the building as they tried to reset the override. Sawyer started the car and they pulled speeding from the parking spot.

Fortunately, the security gate held no barriers besides a mechanical arm. It was lowered to stop traffic, but Sawyer didn't even slow down as he drove straight through it, splintering it into multiple pieces.

Megan looked out the back window and saw the security guard run out of the gatehouse, but there was nothing he could do about the damage now.

"I told them they needed stronger security at the gatehouse," Sawyer muttered, then turned and winked at Megan. "I'll bet they'll listen to me now."

Megan's heart was pounding. "That was really close."

Sawyer reached over and grabbed her hand. "I know. You did great."

"I wasn't sure you'd know when to open the door."

"Well, thankfully, all the men's attention was focused on you—as usual—not on me standing right outside the door. Although I was pretending to be on a phone call in case anyone looked."

Megan ignored the "as usual" part. She had found that men's attention was very rarely directed at her. Well, maybe it had been a few moments ago, since she was putting on the this-is-how-you-become-a-fugitive show, but not normally.

"And that is quite a sucker punch you have there, Dr. Fuller. If you ever want to try a different profession, you might want to look into MMA."

"MMA?"

"Mixed martial arts. You could be in the Ultimate Fighting Championship in no time, if this morning is any indication."

Megan knew Sawyer was trying to make her feel better, but the gravity of what she had just done wasn't lost on her. She had probably just thrown eight years of her professional life away. There was no way she'd be able to go back to Cyberdyne like it was before, no matter how important the countermeasure project was or how many lives she saved. She was a security risk now. And that was something that would follow her even if she moved to a different company.

Her field was a rather close-knit group. Highly competitive with each other, sure, but also chatty. What Megan had just done—stealing company property, assaulting the head of security, tearing through the guard gate as if she was in some sort of *Dukes of Hazzard* episode—would be all over the computer R & D community by the day's end.

Maybe Megan *should* look into a job as an MMA fighter. Because she wasn't going to be working in the computer R & D field anytime soon.

"Are the police going to be after us?"

"Probably. But not right away."

Megan looked over at Sawyer. "Are you going to get in trouble for what just happened?"

Sawyer shrugged, but definitely didn't look overly concerned. "Omega won't like that little stunt with the gate." He cringed a little at that. "But given what happened at your house, your car accident and the evidence of a traitor inside Cyberdyne? No, I'm definitely not going to be in any trouble."

"So what's the plan?"

"First, back to the hotel, where we can pick up everything. Then on to the safe house."

"Do you know where that is yet?"

Sawyer scowled just a bit. "It's not anything close to a lab, like I was requesting. But I guess that's to be expected on such short notice."

"All right, well, a lab isn't critical. I just need somewhere where I can spread out and not have anybody try to kill or arrest me for a while."

Sawyer chucked softly. "Roger that."

Halfway back to the hotel, Sawyer's phone vibrated in the console between them. Sawyer glanced down at the text when they stopped at a red light.

"Okay, slight change of plans," he announced, returning the phone to its place.

"Bad or good?"

"Evidently Omega found us a new safe house. It's farther out of town, but the remote location gives us more room like you wanted and Omega feels it's more secure." Sawyer frowned when he said it.

"But you don't agree?"

"No, they're probably right. Less traffic is probably better. But it won't be ready for a few hours."

There was something else Sawyer wanted to say, it seemed like, but he wasn't talking. Megan knew she shouldn't borrow Sawyer's trouble, too; she had enough to worry about. If there was something that concerned him enough, he would share it.

But Megan couldn't ignore the little nagging pulse in the back of her mind. She'd had it before, usually when she was in the middle of a development project, frustrated because she and the team couldn't get something right.

The certainty that she was missing something. Something important.

Megan could swear that was the case now, but for the life of her couldn't figure out what it was.

She just hoped she figured it out before it was too late.

THAT HAD BEEN too damn close. Now that they were safely in the car and no one was coming after them—that bit he'd told Megan about the cops not coming after them was somewhat of a stretch—Sawyer could relax a little.

When Sawyer saw Ted Cory catch up to Megan, he had thought it was all over. She had handled herself like a champ—more than Sawyer would've expected from almost anybody, even a seasoned agent. The lady definitely had a giant brain, but she wasn't afraid of action. Otherwise, she'd be locked in Cory's office right now threatened with arrest if she didn't provide the countermeasure and Ghost Shell.

It would've set them back from finishing for at least two or three days, possibly much longer. Exactly what DS-13 needed in order to be able to sell their version of Ghost Shell as soon as possible.

Sawyer definitely hadn't counted on Ted Cory being at the office so early and immediately searching for Megan. But Megan had made it out and that was what mattered.

Sawyer needed to call in to Omega and let them know what had happened. He'd told the truth when he'd assured Megan he wouldn't be reprimanded for getting her out; Megan finishing the countermeasure was more important that the security director's rules at a private corporation.

Although Omega definitely wouldn't like the ramming-the-gate thing. Sawyer snickered a little. He'd like to be a fly on the wall when his boss, Dennis Burgamy, got that news.

Sawyer just wanted to get Megan to the safe house so she could finish the countermeasure. This new safe house sounded as if it better suited their needs, which made it fine by Sawyer, although he wished Omega would just pick one place and stick with it. Sawyer didn't like changes when his and other's lives were at stake.

They arrived at the hotel. Sawyer parked around back and they quickly made their way to his room. Where Sawyer stayed wasn't public knowledge, but there weren't many hotels in the small town of Swannanoa and the local police would certainly be patrolling around here before long.

Megan was looking a little shell-shocked. Sawyer led her over to the bed and encouraged her to sit down.

"You okay?" he asked.

"Yes. I just don't know how you do this all the time—the lying and narrowly escaping and running crazy."

Sawyer kissed her forehead. "Believe it or not, my job is not always like that. Or at least the craziness is a little more spread out."

Megan shook her head and sat back. "If you say so."

Sawyer gathered all his items and packed them quickly. It wasn't long before they were leaving, heading out the back just so no one in the lobby would happen to remember seeing them.

Sawyer drove them out of town, the opposite way from where the safe house was located. They needed to get some food, and Sawyer needed to check in. But just in case someone remembered seeing them and were questioned, Sawyer didn't want to be anywhere near where he and Megan would be going.

Sawyer found a diner of the twenty-four-hour variety not too far south of town. He pulled in, keeping an alert eye for anything—or anyone—that might be out of place. But nothing drew his attention. He got Megan into a booth, they both ordered and then Sawyer stepped outside to call in to Omega. He made sure to stay where he could see the booth from the window.

Sawyer dialed the number for Omega, then entered his

personal security code. He waited to be connected to a handler so he could make his report.

"Blowing up a security gate, baby brother? Seriously?"

Sawyer felt himself relax. It wasn't often Juliet ended up as his handler, but since he wasn't technically undercover right now, he didn't have one specific person he was reporting to. She must have seen his code and decided she wanted to take the call.

"Blowing *through*, sis, blowing *through*."

Juliet laughed. "Either way, I'm sure Burgamy is not going to be thrilled when he gets the report."

Sawyer smirked at the thought of his boss hearing about it. "I guess that will teach him to send me on a babysitting job."

"You always seem to find trouble, Sawyer, no matter what you do or where you go."

"It's a gift." Sawyer chuckled. "How did Omega hear about the gate already?"

"Cyberdyne's head of security called and reported your rogue activity."

"And what was he told?"

"The usual—that you were working on orders that were above his security clearance and that sometimes desperate measures are required to complete those orders."

Sawyer was glad Omega had his back. At least he wouldn't have to worry about the local police coming after them. "I hope that's enough to keep Ted Cory from doing something stupid on his own."

"Me, too," Juliet told him. "How is everything going with Dr. Fuller? I heard she ended up being...not what you expected."

Sawyer could hear the smile in his sister's voice. "Where'd you hear that from?" he asked her.

"A little birdie."

"Yeah, well, I imagine that little birdie is about six foot

two with brown hair?" Sawyer had no doubt that Evan was the one telling his secrets. Especially if it was to Juliet. "I thought you didn't talk to Evan very often."

"I don't usually. But he had info about you, so...we talked for a while."

Sawyer didn't want to bring up Evan or any subject that would cause Juliet more pain. She'd been through enough.

Sawyer changed the topic. "I guess this report-in was almost unnecessary since Ted Cory did a lot of it for me. The important thing is I've got Dr. Fuller in pocket and we've got everything she needs to finish the countermeasure on her own."

Sawyer looked into the diner and saw that their food was being delivered. He gestured for Megan to go ahead and eat. "I'll be taking Dr. Fuller to the updated safe house soon."

"How long does she think it will take to complete the countermeasure?" Juliet asked.

"I'm not sure. Less than twenty-four hours, I hope."

"Evan's concerned."

Sawyer nodded. "I know. The timing is going to be pretty tight on this. As soon as the safe house is ready, I'll take Megan there immediately."

"Megan?"

"Dr. Fuller. Don't you give me a hard time about her, too." Sawyer grimaced. "She needs a few hours of sleep, which unfortunately is going to have to happen in the car, I guess. She's been under a lot of stress the last couple of days." Sawyer explained about the accident and break-in at her house. "Plus what happened at her job today."

"You might as well let her sleep, especially if the safe house isn't ready. She'll be able to work much more efficiently if she's firing on all cylinders."

"You're probably right. Thanks, sis."

"Be careful out there, Sawyer. She's not a trained agent."

Sawyer wasn't sure if Juliet was warning him off Megan

on a personal level or just reminding him of the obvious: this entire situation was much harder on Megan than it was on him. Megan didn't have any training or expertise on how to deal with this type of stress. Either way, Sawyer knew he should listen to his sister.

"I hear you, Jules. I'm on a twelve-hour report-in schedule right now, so I'll be calling back in this evening."

"Be safe."

Sawyer hung up and walked back into the diner. Sawyer knew he would do anything necessary to keep Megan safe from DS-13. The question was, who would keep her safe from him?

Chapter Fifteen

A few hours later Sawyer sat in the backseat of his car, his back resting against the door, an exhausted Megan sleeping up against his chest. They had finished their meal and left the diner. With still a couple of hours before the safe house would be ready for them, and Megan close to a breakdown, Sawyer had found a park for them to stop at.

A full stomach made them both feel better, but Sawyer could tell that exhaustion was pulling at Megan. She had been quiet through most of their meal, unfocused, drifting. Sawyer had never seen Megan like that. It looked as if Juliet had been right; the pressure—the entire situation—was proving too much for Megan's system to handle.

Sawyer couldn't do much about the pressure, but he could give her a couple hours' rest so she could hopefully reset. He had no doubt she could get the job done if she could just rest for a while. Even giant brains had to shut down sometime.

When they'd stopped at the park, it had taken Megan long moments to even realize they weren't moving anymore. She turned and looked blankly over at Sawyer.

"Hey, sweetheart. We're going to stop here for a while and let you rest."

"Where are we?"

"A park. But a good one where we can be partially hidden and I can see if anyone is coming."

"Is it safe for us to sleep?"

"You're going to sleep. I'm going to be watching out while you do."

"But are you okay? Don't you need sleep, too?"

Even after all she had been through, exhaustion clear in her features, she was still concerned about him. Sawyer shook his head and ran a finger down her cheek. "I'm fine, hon. It's time for you to rest now."

Megan had gotten into the backseat and stretched out, almost instantly falling asleep. Sawyer had remained in the front. Even in her sleep, Megan couldn't get comfortable, shifting around back and forth. Sawyer realized she was shivering. The temperature outside the car was dropping and sitting here in a running car would be pretty conspicuous.

Sawyer didn't have a blanket, but he definitely had his own body heat. He could be on guard just as easily from the backseat as the front. Removing his Sig from his shoulder holster, he kept it in his hand as he got out of the car and slid into the backseat.

Megan hadn't even awakened when he shifted her slight weight so she was sleeping up against him. But she had cuddled into his warmth. Sawyer had circled her with one arm and kept a watchful eye out for any enemies who might approach, although he doubted DS-13 would be looking for them in a park.

He hadn't minded holding Megan against him for those hours while she slept, keeping her safe. Of course, having her snuggle and rub up against him constantly was pretty much torture. But Sawyer found he didn't care if it meant Megan could get what she needed.

A first for him, he could admit. Sawyer loved women.

Loved their softness and their idiosyncrasies and their beauty that came in all shapes and sizes.

But Sawyer wasn't a man who just tended to hold one while she slept when there were other things—and in this case, he could think of quite a few detailed other things—he'd rather be doing with her. But right now he was content to just hold Megan against him and listen to the adorable little snore that escaped her tiny frame every once in a while.

It must be this case that was causing Sawyer to act so out of character. The case had almost killed both his brothers last month. So solving it was obviously of abounding importance to Sawyer's subconscious.

Yeah. He'd just keep clinging to that thought and not the thought that he couldn't get this tiny, giant-brained woman out of his mind.

As if on cue, her brown eyes fluttered open. She smiled sleepily at him and stretched. Sawyer grimaced as the entire length of her body was pressed against his.

Then her brain caught up to her body and she stiffened. Obviously, she had just realized that she was all but lying on top of him.

"Feel better after your nap?" Sawyer asked, turning her a little so she was more firmly resting against his chest.

"I can't believe how much better I feel. Although, um, wasn't I back here by myself when I first went to sleep?"

"You were shivering and couldn't get comfortable, so I got back here with you."

"Oh." Megan looked up at him and smiled softly. "Thank you. How long have I been out?"

"About four hours."

"Oh, wow. You know in nap cycles, sleeping ninety to one hundred twenty minutes allows for all the sleep cycles to be completed including REM and deep slow-wave sleep. This allows your mind to return to a state of *replenishment*..."

Sawyer listened, smiling and shaking his head, until she

finished her thoughts about naps, then kissed her. Because unlike sleep cycles and brain activity, kissing her had been on his mind for the past four hours.

Every time he kissed her he figured that it couldn't be as good as he remembered it. And every time he was wrong. It was always this good.

Megan sighed and snuggled closer to him. Sawyer placed his Sig on the floor and reached down, grabbing Megan's hips and pulling her closer. Her head slanted to the side and her lips opened, giving Sawyer fuller access. Her tongue dueled with his, hesitantly at first, then with more boldness. Sawyer felt Megan's hands slide up into his hair, gripping hard. He pulled her closer.

And cursed the fact that they were in the backseat of a car, in an open area. And that just because DS-13 hadn't found them yet didn't mean they weren't searching.

And that this was a park, for God's sake. If they didn't stop they might scar some poor little kid for life.

But despite all that, Sawyer didn't want to stop. He definitely didn't want to.

"Megan…" he murmured against her lips.

"I know. I know. We have to stop."

"Believe me, I don't want to. But it's not safe and damn it, I don't want our first time to be in the back of a car like a couple of teenagers."

Megan giggled slightly at that.

Sawyer kissed her lightly again. "But I want you to understand something, Dr. Fuller. Soon. Very, very soon—" he rested his forehead against hers "—we are going to finish what we started here. And when we do, there won't be any break-ins or parks or anything else in the way. It will be in a bed where there is no one around but you and me."

A COUPLE OF hours later, stopped again for a meal, Megan felt much better. She was ready to get on to the safe house and finish the countermeasure. After everything DS-13 had cost her—her home, her vehicle, her possessions, her job—it was time to make them pay for a change. Finishing the countermeasure would do that.

She looked across the booth at Sawyer. She also wanted to get to the safe house so she could finish what she had started with him.

Megan barely refrained from licking her lips thinking about it. And the glances she caught Sawyer giving her every once in a while weren't helping. As if he was considering crawling over the table to get to her.

It made Megan giddy. And she loved it. But at the same time she was well aware that this was Sawyer's MO. He was probably always this focused on women he was attracted to. She'd do well not to read anything more into it than what it meant: a good time for however long he was here.

Hey, she'd take it. If there was one thing all the craziness of the past couple of days had taught her, it was not to waste time worrying so much over the future that you were completely blind to the present sitting right across from you smiling.

But now that her brain wasn't so exhausted, that little nagging bit of her subconscious was back. Nothing about Sawyer. She knew it wasn't about him. But Megan couldn't shake the feeling she was missing something and it was starting to make her twitchy.

"What's wrong?" Sawyer asked her.

"What?"

"You've got that look. Your I'm-using-my-giant-brain-to-figure-out-something-important look."

Megan laughed a little at that. "My subconscious is tugging at me. I've missed something, somewhere, but I don't know what it is."

"About the countermeasure?"

"No, not really. At least, I don't think so." Megan took another bite of her food. "But it's something important."

"Okay. What can I do to help?"

Megan shrugged one shoulder. "I don't know that you can do anything. I've learned to just leave it alone—the harder I try to figure it out, the more elusive it seems to become. It'll come to me."

Megan just hoped it wouldn't come to her too late to be of any use.

They finished eating and headed back out to the car. Megan was ready to get to the safe house and get started. Sawyer was tense in the car, constantly looking in the rear-view mirror.

"Is somebody following us?"

"No." Sawyer shook his head, but didn't look over at her. "I just want to make sure. In such a remote area, it's critical that no one be following us when we reach the safe house."

Twice Sawyer turned off the main road in a direction opposite from where they were trying to go. He drove for just a few moments, then turned and went back the other way. Anyone following them would've been obvious. Megan mentioned that to Sawyer.

Sawyer shook his head. "They're only obvious if they are the only car following us. If I was DS-13 trying to follow our car, I'd have more than one vehicle. Tag-teaming makes a tail much less noticeable."

That made sense to Megan. Still, she didn't see how anybody could follow them, and not be obvious, the way Sawyer drove.

Eventually, after at least thirty minutes out of their way and back, Sawyer felt secure no one was following them. Megan could see him relax, which made her feel better.

He reached over and plucked her hand out of her lap and brought it to his lips, kissing the back of her palm. "Sorry. I don't mean to be fanatic. I just don't want to take a chance with your safety."

Megan smiled. "I understand and appreciate it. Of course, I have no idea where we are."

"Don't worry, I have the address encrypted on my phone. I got a message earlier this morning with the info from Omega."

Something in how Sawyer said the words jarred loose what her subconscious had been trying to get at: *I got a message earlier.*

"Sawyer, stop the car," Megan told him. "I remember. What I couldn't figure out before, I remember."

To his credit, Sawyer didn't hesitate or brush her off. He immediately pulled the car over at a nearby gas station, but parked far away from the building and pumps.

"What?" Sawyer asked her. "Is it something bad?"

"It was something Ted Cory said this morning. Everything happened so fast when he grabbed me that I didn't really put it together it until now."

"What did he say?"

"When you talked to him on the phone while we were in the hotel this morning, you told him I wasn't coming in until the afternoon, right?"

"Yeah. I tried to buy us some extra time."

"But then you reported in to Omega that we were going in this morning to retrieve the needed items, right? Omega and you and I were the only ones who knew we would be there early this morning, right?"

Sawyer nodded. "Yes, but I don't understand what you're getting at."

Megan turned and faced Sawyer fully. "The very first thing Ted Cory said to me as I was trying to get out the door at Cyberdyne was, 'I got a message that you would be here this morning.'"

Sawyer leaned his head back against the seat, obviously

processing what Megan was telling him. "You're sure he said 'I got a message' not 'I thought you'd probably be here' or something like that?"

"I'm positive. I can recall the entire conversation word for word if you want." Megan tapped her finger against her temple. It was the truth. She could recall probably the past one hundred conversations she'd had almost word for word. It had just taken her subconscious a little time to put together that Ted Cory's words were important in an unusual way.

"No need. I believe you." Sawyer ran a hand over his eyes.

"Does this mean what I think it means?"

Sawyer clenched his jaw visibly. "It means everything is blown to hell, that's what it means."

Chapter Sixteen

Damn it, Sawyer wanted to punch something. He had thought there might be someone involved from Omega, but hadn't wanted to believe it. Now the truth was too obvious to ignore.

Somebody had contacted Ted Cory and warned him that Megan would be coming in this morning, despite what Sawyer had told Cory. That was why he had been there so early. It was probably why Trish Wilborne—if she was the Cyberdyne traitor—was there so early, also. It made sense.

It also meant nothing involving Omega was trustworthy anymore. Including the safe house.

Or the car they were driving. Or the phone Sawyer had.

Sawyer immediately opened the car door.

"Where are we going?" Megan asked.

"Hang on just a second," he told her.

Sawyer stayed seated, but set his phone on the ground outside the car, then shut the door again.

"To answer your earlier question, yes, it does mean what you think it means. Someone inside Omega is working against us, too."

"And you put your phone outside because you think they're using it to track us."

Sawyer grimaced. "If it's someone using Omega's resources, they're almost definitely using it to track us. I put it outside because a smartphone can also be used as a transmitting device with the right technology."

"Should you destroy it?" Megan was starting to get that pinched look again. Sawyer hated that, but couldn't blame her.

"I might. But not until we come up with a plan." Sawyer hit the steering wheel with the bottom of his fist. "No wonder they weren't tailing us. They didn't need to. They knew where we were going."

"Do you think they planned to wait until we got to the safe house, then ambush us?"

Sawyer ran tense fingers through his hair. "Definitely, if not worse."

"What are we going to do?"

That was the million-dollar question. Sawyer still needed to get Megan to a safe location so she could finish the countermeasure. But with the resources Omega had, staying hidden from the mole would be difficult, if not impossible.

Omega would be able to trace any car he and Megan tried to rent. If Sawyer stole one, Omega would be able to access traffic and security cameras from all around. They also had local law enforcement on their side.

When Omega wanted to hunt someone down, especially when they knew the general location and description of that someone, it was damn near impossible to get away.

The first thing Sawyer knew he needed to do was get some reinforcements on his side. He needed to call Juliet and let her know what was going on. The only way he could do that safely would be on a pay phone.

"Okay, I'm going to open the car door and get my phone and leave it in the car as we get out. Don't say anything until we are both outside of the car and the phone is inside," he told Megan.

"They can hear us even with it powered down?"

"It's my Omega phone. A mole there could've had access and modified it to transmit."

"Kind of like some new technology that's being used by people who think their spouses might be having an affair."

Sawyer nodded. "In essence."

Megan shook her head. "Do you have a plan?"

"I'm going to call someone in Omega I know I can trust, my sister, Juliet. She'll have access to information we need."

They both were silent as they got out of the car and Sawyer put the phone inside. Then they walked over to a pay phone on the side of the gas station. Sawyer dialed Juliet's number. When she picked up, he didn't let her get many words out. "Hey, sis. Our stepmom just called and told me there's a huge sale down at the local coffeehouse."

There was a short pause. "Really? That's awesome."

"Yeah, she said you might want to bring your computer so you can research which coffee to buy."

"Alrighty, then. I'll go check it out and call you back."

They both hung up. Megan was looking at him as if he'd lost his mind.

"Do I even want to know?" she asked him. "Please tell me that was some kind of code."

Sawyer smiled. "We don't have a stepmom. Our parents are still happily married and live in Virginia. *Stepmom* is kind of a family code for 'get someplace where you can talk privately.'"

It wasn't long before Juliet was calling him back. "What's up, Sawyer? This better be worth me going outside in this weather. It's cold."

"Are you somewhere that you can talk without anyone from Omega overhearing?"

"Yeah. I'm totally out of the building."

"We've got a big problem, Juliet. Megan figured out that someone at Omega is working against us."

"Damn it, I knew it!"

That wasn't the response Sawyer was expecting from his sister at all.

"You did? Why the hell didn't you tell me, then?"

Juliet backtracked. "Well, I didn't know for sure. But I was looking up the info on the safe house you're going to— Evan wanted to know where you'd be exactly."

Sawyer didn't mind Evan Karcz knowing the safe-house location. Evan wasn't actual family, but he was close enough. Although, if Sawyer had to guess, Evan had only asked about the safe house in order to get Juliet to talk to him, not just because he wanted to be aware of Sawyer's location.

"Evan's questions made you think there was someone working against us?"

"No. I went into the system to get him the address. Found it no problem."

Sawyer rubbed his face with this hand. "Juliet, I don't get what you're talking about."

"I was prepared to filter through addresses because you had mentioned being given a second address. But there was only one in the system."

"Okay. But that still doesn't necessarily mean—"

"Sawyer, there was no record *anywhere* of a first address. The second—the more remote location—was the only one attached to your case. If you hadn't mentioned you'd been given a second, different safe-house location, I wouldn't have looked twice at the file."

"Is it possible it was a clerical error?"

"No. Once I went back and found your call-in record from last night, I was able to trace the original safe house assigned to you. Someone deliberately went in and deleted all record of that assignment, so it looked like the second safe house was the one originally assigned."

Sawyer was silent. He didn't want to let his imagination get the better of him, but the only reasons he could think of for someone to make it look as if the second house had been originally assigned was for some definite nefarious purposes. "That's bad."

"It's very bad, Sawyer. It looks like someone is pre-emptively covering their tracks. The only reason I can think that someone would do that—"

"Is if they were going to take Megan and me out of the picture entirely, then make it look like an accident or attack from DS-13 or something." Sawyer finished Juliet's idea for her. He heard a slight gasp from Megan and turned to look at her. Her eyes were giant as she looked at him.

"You can't go to that safe house, Sawyer."

"I know, sis, but neither can we run if someone's got Omega's resources to use when looking for us. We won't get far."

"I assume you don't have your phone within earshot. Remember, it can be used not only to track you, but for remote listening."

"No, it's sitting inside the car. I didn't want to destroy it, hoping we'll be able to use their own system against them. Feed them false info while they're listening in."

"Okay, but don't say anything around it you don't want overheard. Even if it's off," Juliet continued.

"Okay, got it." Sawyer told her.

"Do you want me to take the information I have to Burgamy, or even higher up?"

"No, we don't know who the traitor is. I don't want to take a chance on notifying the wrong person." Sawyer looked down at Megan, who was standing next to Sawyer so she could hear as much as possible. Sawyer hated the thought that someone in law enforcement had lied and put her in jeopardy *again*. He grabbed her hands, which were clenched tightly in front of her, gently running his finger over her knuckles.

"Sawyer." Juliet spoke and got his attention again. "I think I'm coming up with a plan."

If there was one thing his sister was known for, it was strategic planning.

"Megan needs time and a quiet place to work, right?"

"Yes, and the sooner the better."

"Evan is out in that area. You call in to Omega and let them know you can't get to the safe house right away for some reason. I'll have Evan check out the safe house, see if there's anything interesting to be found. Meanwhile I'll keep poking around here."

"And then what?"

"Well, if we find what I think we might find, it's going to prove that DS-13, and whoever is helping them at Omega, have decided if they can't keep you in-pocket then dead is an acceptable alternative."

If possible, Megan turned even paler at Juliet's words. "What exactly are we going to do about that, Jules?" Sawyer asked his sister.

"Give them what they want."

A FEW HOURS later they got the confirmation Sawyer had been dreading. A text came in on Megan's phone, telling them to call Aunt Susie when they got a chance. Since Megan didn't have an Aunt Susie, they figured out Juliet had news for them.

They had spent the past few hours driving around. Sawyer had made two calls in to Omega. The first, immediately after the conversation with Juliet, to tell them he thought they were being followed and therefore wouldn't be going to the safe house. The other about an hour ago to say they were stopping at a supercenter for some items Megan needed due to the break-in. Which was true—they had stopped to get a few things.

Most important, clean, untraceable phones that could

be used once Sawyer stopped using his current one to feed false info to Omega.

But generally they were just stalling and it would become obvious soon, so Sawyer was thankful to see his sister's text.

But he definitely wasn't thankful for the news.

"Evan found explosives, Sawyer," Juliet told him when they stopped at a payphone and called a few minutes later. "He's on the other line with us."

"Somebody's definitely trying to take you out," Evan stated, seriousness evident in his tone. "But all home-baked stuff, nothing that would raise red flags in an arson investigation. Given the location—a remote building, non-residential neighborhood—it looks like someone might be trying to make it look like an accident." Evan explained a few more details.

The expletive that came out of Sawyer's mouth was not one he would normally use around his sister, or any woman. "If DS-13 is willing to kill Megan, then things have just gone from bad to hell-in-a-handbasket. Especially if they've got Omega's resources at their disposal."

Sawyer wrapped an arm around Megan, pulling her closer to him. He needed to get them off the street as soon as possible. But they wouldn't be able to hide for long.

"I think your plan is the best one, Juliet," he told his sister.

"What plan?" Evan asked.

"Megan and I are going to give them what they want. We'll go to the safe house and make them think we're staying. But we'll get out immediately. They'll blow it up like they planned and will think we're dead. But we'll be gone."

Evan chuckled wryly. "Juliet, your plans get more crazy each time."

"Hey, my crazy plans have saved your life more than once, Evan."

"I'm going to need you to have a car waiting for us there, Evan," Sawyer interrupted. "And once we leave the not-safe safe house, we'll need a hotel in Asheville."

"This won't hold them off forever, Sawyer," Juliet told him. "It won't take long for the official arson report to read that no bodies were present. I can probably stall the report, but not for long. This whole stunt will only buy you forty-eight hours, tops."

Sawyer looked down questioningly at Megan, who was standing close enough to listen to the conversation. She nodded.

"Forty-eight hours will be enough. It has to be."

Chapter Seventeen

Megan felt as though the world was spinning at a pace out of her control. Having someone after the countermeasure, even wrecking her car and breaking in to her house felt like a game compared to this.

DS-13 was trying to kill them.

Megan had sat mostly silent for the past few hours as Sawyer had fed misinformation to his workplace and formulated plans with his team. Plans to escape, evade, misdirect. But most importantly, survive.

On one hand, Megan could appreciate the logistical nature of what they were doing—the elaborate planning going into all of it. It wasn't unlike the projects she worked on and developed for Cyberdyne. It all had to fit together perfectly to work. The planning appealed to her giant brain, as Sawyer so loved to call it.

But on the other hand, Megan was just downright frightened. She hadn't said much of anything today because of Sawyer's phone possibly being used to transmit data. What if Megan accidentally said something that gave away important information about the plan? What if she blurted out something about traitors?

Better to keep as quiet as possible.

Megan wrapped her arms around her midsection, not sure if she might fly apart any second.

She was outside, sitting on the trunk of the car. Sawyer's phone was inside, so there was no need to monitor their statements for the moment.

Sawyer had removed all the countermeasure equipment from the backseat and was carefully packing it in two backpacks. They'd need to travel a couple of miles carrying the equipment, to get to the vehicle Evan had left for them.

"Once we get inside the house, you need to immediately announce you want to sleep," Sawyer told her, not looking up from his careful packing. He was in full mission mode. "I'll say that I'm going to unwind for a couple of hours and unpack, and mention that we won't plan on leaving the safe house for multiple days."

Megan nodded.

"Once we get the house dark, we'll immediately want to leave. I don't know when they'll trigger the explosives. Evan says it's on a remote detonator, so it can be detonated from anywhere."

"Sawyer." Megan hardly recognized her own voice. "How do we know they won't set off the explosives as soon as we walk into the house?"

Sawyer stopped packing and stood, walking over to Megan and standing right in front of her. "That is a possibility." He unwrapped her arms from around her stomach and put them on his shoulders instead. "But it is far more likely that they will wait until we are more settled in for the night. Especially if they're trying to make it look like an accident. Plus, if the mole doesn't want to blow his own cover, it will be much less suspicious if the building doesn't blow up ten seconds after we walk in."

He kissed her briefly, gently.

Megan could agree with the logic of his statement, and the odds. But she was still not thrilled about the thought of them walking into a building—even just for a few minutes—designed to kill them. But it didn't look as if there were many other options.

Sawyer kissed her again and went back to packing. Once the backpacks were ready, he placed them in paper grocery bags. He noticed Megan's raised eyebrow.

"To make it look like we're planning to stay in the house for a while, in case someone's watching. Got to have groceries."

"Oh, right." There was so much Sawyer thought of that hadn't even crossed her mind. Megan was obviously not cut out for subterfuge.

Sawyer placed the grocery bags in the backseat, then helped Megan down from her perch. He walked her around to the passenger-side door, opening it for her and helping her inside. Megan couldn't help but smile, although she knew it was tense.

"Are we on a date?"

Sawyer winked at her. "Not yet, but soon. Believe me, you'll know when I have you out for a date."

Despite all the tension, Megan's heart gave a little jump.

Sawyer walked around to the driver's side and grabbed his phone. He texted Omega, letting them know he and Megan were heading to the safe house. The sun was setting, providing them the darkness they would use to sneak out before the bomb went off.

They hoped.

Megan wrapped her arms around herself again, stomach twisted even tighter. A lot could go wrong in the next couple of hours. All of which would have the same result: Sawyer's and Megan's deaths.

Sawyer put the phone down, his message sent. This was it, the plan was in place whether Megan was ready or not.

Sawyer glanced over at her, concerned. Given the way Megan was manually attempting to keep her body functioning, she couldn't blame him for his concern.

"Okay, this is it. You ready?"

"No offense intended, but I don't really have much of a choice, do I?" Megan tried to force herself to relax, but couldn't.

Sawyer shook his head. "No, neither of us has much of a choice. Let's get to the safe house so you can get a little rest then get started."

Megan remembered someone was listening, so she went back to being silent. It wasn't long before they reached their destination.

The building itself wasn't what Megan was expecting, although if she was honest, she couldn't pinpoint exactly what she had been expecting. A haunted mansion, perhaps? Complete with gargoyles?

It was just a small garage/workshop that looked as if it had some sort of living quarters on the top. It backed up against a body of water—maybe a small lake? Megan couldn't be sure in the darkness. Trees and bushes surrounded it, but no other houses or buildings.

That was good—at least nobody would be hurt by the explosion. Megan hoped the same would be true for her and Sawyer.

"Okay, this is it. I'm going to open that garage door so we can park inside."

Sawyer had to manually open the garage door, an old-fashioned kind that swung out like a traditional door, instead of up. He pulled the car in and closed the door behind them.

As she watched the door close, Megan fought to keep her panic in check. The walls seemed to be closing in around her. She could only think, *Are we about to die any second?*

Megan jumped when Sawyer opened the backseat door to remove the "grocery" bags. He raised an eyebrow at her, then gestured with a circular motion of his hand for her to breathe. Megan closed her eyes and took a deep breath letting it out slowly.

She had to keep it together. If she started sobbing right now, the whole ruse would be up, not to mention might cause whoever was listening to trigger the bomb.

Megan forced herself to get out of the car and she and Sawyer walked up the stairs into the living quarters together.

"This isn't as bad as I thought it might be, although a few windows might be nice." Megan stood right in the middle of the small living room, unsure where to go.

"Glad it meets your approval, because we're going to be here awhile."

Megan didn't want to draw out the conversation in case someone was trigger-happy. "I'm really tired. I'd like to sleep for a while before I start work on the countermeasure."

It was almost word for word what Sawyer had told her to say. Megan wasn't much of an actress.

"That's fine." Sawyer nodded. "I'm going to unpack this stuff and just hang out."

Megan went into the bedroom and turned on the light, walked around a little, went into the bathroom for a while, then came back out and turned off the light. Following the script Sawyer had provided almost down to the letter. Megan heard the TV come on and knew he was doing the same.

Megan lay down on top of the bed. After long moments, Sawyer came into the room, keeping to the shadows, both backpacks in hand.

"Are you ready?" he asked her in a voice barely over a whisper.

Megan nodded.

"My phone is by the television speaker, so I doubt anyone can hear us now," Sawyer continued. "We're going to need to go back down the stairs and out the garage door.

This place, with hardly any usable windows and only one door, has got to be a fire hazard. Somebody picked it well, if they were trying to trap us."

"I didn't even see a window."

"It's downstairs and pretty small. I'm not surprised you didn't notice it. I don't know if anyone is actually watching the house or not, but we've got to keep low. Even once we're outside, try to blend in to the trees as much as possible."

"Okay," Megan whispered.

They each slipped on their backpacks and made it to the bottom of the stairs. Once back in the garage, Sawyer motioned for her to stop.

"I just want to see these explosives for myself." He walked over to a corner, shifted a few boxes and lifted a blanket.

If that was the bomb, it wasn't like anything Megan had seen in the movies. It just looked like a couple of fertilizer bags stacked on top of each other, with some cans around it. The only thing even mildly suspicious about it was the really old notebook computer sitting on top of it.

"Ammonium nitrate. Surrounded by paint thinner and gas. All stuff you'd expect at a place this old and remote. Suggesting it was an accident wouldn't be far-fetched."

"What is that computer?"

"The timing mechanism. Most of it will get burned away, but if any of it is found, nobody will think much of it."

The screen of the old laptop booted on, startling them both.

Sawyer muttered an expletive, then grabbed Megan's shoulders and pushed her forward in front of him, toward the large garage door. "Go, go!"

Megan got to the door and began to push it. It wouldn't budge.

"Sawyer, I can't get it to move."

Without a word Sawyer came around in front of her

and put his shoulder to the door. She heard his curse when he couldn't get it to move, either. It was completely stuck.

Sawyer grabbed Megan's hand and ran to the window in the back of the garage. He used a hammer to break the glass and used the side of it to clear the glass from the sill, and ripped off both their backpacks.

"That laptop screen coming on means that something has happened with the remote trigger. It could go off any second." Sawyer was already hoisting Megan through the window as he said it.

Now that Megan understood, she didn't waste time asking questions. She scrambled through the window, falling the few feet to the ground on the other side.

She immediately got back up, catching the backpacks as Sawyer threw them out in front of him. The brisk air surrounded her, time moving in slow motion, as Sawyer deftly began to make his own way through the window.

Until he got stuck. Megan watched as his large shoulders were jammed in the sill.

"Megan, I need you to run." He said it to her as he attempted to back out and resituate himself.

"No. I can help you."

"Megan, just go now. Take the equipment with you. If this building goes up, then what you've done with countermeasure has to make it out of here."

She ran over to him and tried to help as Sawyer struggled to fit through the window. "It's not more important than your life."

"Megan, look at me." Megan stopped her frantic pulling at his shoulders. "No offense, but the countermeasure is more important than either of our lives. Please go."

Megan felt tears streaming down her face, but she understood what Sawyer was saying. If the bomb went off right now, both of them would die and the countermeasure would be totally destroyed.

Megan grabbed both backpacks and began running. She looked back at Sawyer, but he had disappeared back inside the window.

Damn it, she was not leaving him to die some fiery death; she didn't care what he said about the importance of the countermeasure. She dropped the bags far enough away that they would be safe, then circled back to the house. The window was too small; she'd never be able to help him out of that.

But something was blocking the garage door in front. Maybe she could get it out of the way.

She ran around to the front of the building knowing that if someone was watching them, it was going to ruin Juliet's brilliant plan of faking their deaths. Of course, if she and Sawyer both died, the plan was also ruined. She hoped that whoever had blocked the door was gone, although she kept to the shadows on the off chance that it would help.

A crowbar had been lodged in the double-door handles— a simple but effective means of trapping people inside. And an explosion would certainly knock the doors off their hinges or burn them completely—still making an accident look feasible.

Megan slid the heavy door open just a tiny bit and stuck her head inside.

"Sawyer!"

He was over by the pile of ammonium nitrate.

"Megan? What the hell are you doing here?"

"I've got the door unblocked. Just come on."

Sawyer ran as fast as he could toward her. "I was trying to defuse this, but couldn't. The computer is counting down. We've only got a few seconds."

He grabbed her hand as they rushed out the door, sprinting for the trees. Megan could hear a loud sizzling noise behind her, but didn't look back.

Even knowing the explosion was coming, the force of

it surprised her. There was a bright light before heat and pressure threw her to the ground. She felt Sawyer slide his body over to protect hers from any debris. Twigs and branches flew everywhere.

Once it seemed safe, they both turned from where they lay and looked back at the damage. Megan gasped. Flames shot high in the building, the garage already completely collapsed. No one in that building would've survived.

Sawyer dragged her into his arms. "Your brain has been officially demoted to huge rather than giant after that stunt. You could've been killed."

"Whatever. Like you wouldn't have done the same thing."

Sawyer chuckled at that. "Let's get out of here."

Chapter Eighteen

They circled around to the backpacks, then hiked to the car Evan had left for them. Sawyer was still pretty mad at Megan for risking her life like that, but had to admit she had saved his, so he couldn't be too angry.

At this point Sawyer wasn't sure if their plan to fake their deaths had worked or not. Someone had obviously been at the house, as evidenced by the crowbar wedged in the garage door. Whether that person had stuck around and was able to see them coming out or had left to avoid the first responders who had arrived not long after the explosion, Sawyer didn't know.

Regardless, it didn't change their plans. Everything that tied him to Omega—car, cell phone, even his clothes—had been left in that burning building. There was no way anyone could track them using those items now. Sawyer used the new phones he had bought at the supercenter yesterday to text Juliet and let her know that they'd made it out.

Sawyer drove around for a while to try to make sure no one was following them, then headed to the prearranged and prepaid motel. Evan and Juliet had picked a good one for them, on the other side of Asheville. Sawyer could park directly in front of the door, just steps away from their room if they needed to leave in a hurry.

It was an end unit, so no one would be passing his and

Megan's room to get to their own. There should be no one around at all. Just the way they needed it to be.

Sawyer backed the nondescript car into the parking spot outside their room. He grabbed the backpacks out of the backseat and handed them to Megan, then grabbed the bags of supplies—real food and clothes—Evan had left for them. Sawyer took one last look around as he shut the car door. There seemed to be nothing around them in the darkness, except the Blue Ridge Mountains looming nearby. He led Megan to the room and opened it with the key Evan had left for them.

Sawyer put down the bags and immediately looked around the room. It was actually two adjoining rooms; Megan would need all of one room to finish her work. The motel was definitely older, as evidenced by the actual metal key Sawyer had just used to get in, but clean and adequate for their needs. Plus there was a window in the back that could be used for emergency escape.

Not that Sawyer really wanted to be trying to fit through any windows again.

Sawyer pulled the blinds completely closed in both rooms, and locked and bolted both doors after placing the do-not-disturb sign on both doorknobs. This was it, their home for the next few days.

Sawyer turned and found Megan standing exactly where he'd left her just inside the door. She still cradled both backpacks in her arms.

She looked exhausted. She stood there, covered in dirt from their most recent brush with death, gazing at the motel room without really seeing it. Given everything that had happened to her over the past few days, Sawyer was amazed she had remained upright and functional this long.

Sawyer walked over and took the bags from Megan's unresisting arms and laid them down on the table.

"Hey," he whispered to her. "How about a hot shower?

Get some of this grunge washed off you." Sawyer led her to the bed and sat her down, then went and turned on the hot water in the shower. When he came out of the bathroom, she still sat exactly where he had left her.

Concern flooded Sawyer. What Megan had been through over the past few days would be physically exhausting and emotionally draining for even the most seasoned agent. For a civilian with no experience in this sort of work at all? Sawyer could barely imagine the toll it was taking.

And then to ask her to tackle the countermeasure development on top of all that had happened? Sawyer wasn't even sure it was possible for her, but he had to try.

He crouched beside where she sat on the bed. "Megan, let's get you in the shower, okay? It will help you feel better."

Megan turned to look at him, but seemed uncomprehending of what he wanted. "Shower," he told her again slowly.

"Sawyer, I don't think I know where I am." The confusion in her voice tore at his heart.

"You're at a motel, sweetheart. Don't worry about that right now. Let's just get you into the shower, okay?"

Megan nodded and Sawyer helped her stand and walk into the bathroom.

"Can you get undressed?" Megan nodded again, but then just stood there staring blankly at the wall.

Okay, time to take matters into his own hands. She obviously wasn't able to even complete simple tasks on her own in her current state of mind.

Sawyer reached over and began unbuttoning Megan's shirt. She looked at him as he did it, but made no move to stop him. He peeled the shirt off her shoulders and dropped it onto the sink, then unhooked her bra and removed it. Sawyer did his damn personal best not to stare at her firm, beautiful breasts.

He knelt down, picking up one of her feet at a time to remove her shoes and socks. She began to lose her balance and grasped his shoulders to keep from toppling over.

Sawyer looked up at her through the steam that was now filling the bathroom. "Just hold on to me."

She nodded once again, but at least there was a little bit of awareness in her eyes now, rather than the scary blankness.

Sawyer swallowed hard as his hands moved to the button and zipper of her jeans. He undid both, then slid them down her legs. Her lacy underwear followed suit and he helped her step out of them.

Sawyer cleared his throat, his breath just shy of ragged. "Okay, into the shower you go." He tested the water and adjusted it so it wouldn't scald her, scooped the shower curtain aside and helped her in.

He heard her sigh when the water hit her and closed the curtain around her oh-so-naked form. He had tried to keep his eyes focused above her neckline as much as possible. But Lord, he was only human.

He had to admit this was the first time he had ever gotten a woman he wanted *this* much naked and then just left her alone.

Yeah, he definitely wanted Megan, but not when she was so traumatized she could barely function.

Hopefully, the shower would help perk her up a little. Help her refocus. "Megan, I'll be right outside the door. If you need anything, just call for me. Okay?"

He heard a murmur of agreement, then headed into the motel room, leaving the door cracked open so he could hear her if she called out.

Sawyer took a couple of breaths. Deep breaths. He needed a cold shower. He sat down on the end of the bed and threw himself backward. It was going to be a long night.

THE SHOWER BROUGHT life back into Megan's veins. Slowly she began to feel again. First the heat from the water spraying down on her, then the realization that she was filthy—small twigs and grass were matted into her hair. She began to work her fingers through her locks to get the mess out.

It felt as if her brain was waking up from hibernation. She remembered the explosion, although she didn't allow herself to dwell on Sawyer almost getting trapped in that building. But then everything after that was a blur. They obviously must have made it to the car, and here she was in a shower in a motel room, so that must have gone as planned, also.

She could even vaguely remember Sawyer helping her take off her clothes, which should embarrass her, but she didn't have the energy for it.

Megan stood in the shower for long minutes. She finally opened the shampoo and washed her hair fully. At least she wasn't quite as zombielike as she was before, although she was still exhausted. After washing the rest of her body and rinsing, she shut the water off.

"Doing okay in there?" she heard Sawyer call out from the room.

"Yes, much better. Thanks." She opened the shower curtain and found the door to the bedroom still open. In the mirror she could see Sawyer lying on the bed, propped up on his elbows. His eyes met hers. Megan almost snatched the shower curtain over to cover herself, but figured Sawyer had already seen her naked, so there wasn't much point in it now. She watched as his eyes slid down her body and back up.

The exhaustion that filled her body moments before now vanished. All of her senses seemed heightened.

Sawyer stood up from the bed, keeping eye contact with her. He grabbed a T-shirt—one of his—and threw it over his shoulder, walking to the bathroom. He offered her his hand and she stepped out of the tub onto the mat. Sawyer took a towel from the wall hook and shook it out, then wrapped it around her like a cape, keeping hold of the edges.

Megan said nothing, just continued to stare at Sawyer. He took the edges of the towel and gently dried her face and the excess water from her hair. Then he began to wrap the edges of the towel around his fists, pulling her closer. He didn't stop until she was fully pressed up against him.

"I'm wet," Megan whispered.

"I don't care," Sawyer responded before bringing his lips down to hers.

Sawyer had kissed her before, but this was different. Megan had no doubt how this kiss was going to end. Her bones felt as though they were melting. Everything about this felt right.

After a few minutes, both of them breathing hard, Sawyer released her lips. He used the towel to dry the rest of her body, kneeling in front of her and kissing various areas as he went along. A sigh escaped Megan as his lips made their way across her belly and dipped lower to the outside of her hips.

But then Sawyer stood up and pulled the T-shirt off his shoulder and began to put it on her.

"Um, Sawyer? I think this," she whispered as she gestured to the shirt he was pulling over her head, "is not going in the correct direction."

Sawyer's voice was more husky than usual when he responded, "Believe me, there is nothing I want to do more than take you to that bed. Right now. But fifteen minutes ago you couldn't even remember how you got here."

"But—"

Sawyer put a finger up to her lips. "Later. I promise. Later. But right now, you need to rest. Plus, I'm filthy."

He pulled the shirt over her head and she put her arms through. The shirt swallowed her, falling to midthigh.

"I'm pretty damn sure I never looked that good in that shirt."

Megan smiled and followed as he led her to the room. He pulled back the covers of the bed and she scooted in. "Sleep. I'm going to take a shower, then I'll be sleeping right next to you."

He turned and walked back into the bathroom. And didn't even look back once.

Megan lay on the bed for a long time, but sleep was a million miles away. She knew her body needed sleep, but she needed Sawyer more. At one time she would've let Sawyer's choice to shower fill her with doubts: maybe he didn't really want her, maybe he didn't feel this same attraction the way she did.

But she wasn't going to let that happen right now. She had seen the way Sawyer looked at her. He wanted her, too. And the fact that he was gentleman enough not to want to take any sort of advantage of her because she'd had a rough few days? Honestly, that just made her want him more.

Sawyer had almost died tonight in that building. Megan still felt a tightness in her chest when she pictured the moment he realized he couldn't get through that window.

So, yes, Megan could admit she was exhausted and definitely wasn't used to the level of…excitement the past few days had provided. But she wasn't going to waste any more time with Sawyer.

Sleep could damn well wait. She wanted him now.

Megan had never been particularly forward in her love life, but she wasn't going to let that stop her now, either. She climbed out of bed, pulled his shirt over her head and dropped it. Then walked into the bathroom.

She paused for just a moment, then slid the shower curtain open. Sawyer was facing the showerhead, facedown, arms braced on the wall in front of him. Megan's breath hitched as she watched as the water poured down his muscled back—and beyond.

Finally she reached out and touched him gently on his back, but then snatched her hand away. The water was so cold.

At her touch he turned sharply to look at her. She hadn't meant to startle him.

"Sawyer, I didn't mean to use up all the hot water. I'm so sorry." Megan was distressed at the thought that he'd had to take a cold shower because of her inconsideration.

But Sawyer gave her that half smile that made her insides melt. He reached out with one arm and put her hand on his chest, using his other hand to fiddle with the water controls. Immediately hotter water began pouring down his body and her hand.

"Cold shower by choice," Sawyer said to her, his voice husky. "It was the only way I was going to be able to get into that bed next to you, knowing you weren't wearing anything but my T-shirt."

He looked down her naked body, one eyebrow raised. "Although you seem to have misplaced that."

Megan laughed softly as Sawyer turned off the shower. "I did. I can be pretty absentminded sometimes."

"Fortunately for you I have a particular soft spot for absentminded scientists who end up naked in my bathroom."

Megan walked the few steps to take a clean towel from the rack. "That happens a lot to you, does it?"

"All the time. But usually they're old, gray-haired guys and I tell them to go put their clothes back on."

Megan laughed, but it faded quickly as Sawyer stepped out of the shower, gloriously unconcerned about his nakedness. Megan still had the towel clutched in her hands. She thought about handing it to Sawyer, but instead opened

it and took the few steps that separated them. She began
drying his chest.

"Megan, I just want you to be sure about this," Sawyer whispered, his face only a few inches from hers as
she slowly rubbed the towel across his chest and stomach.
"Just because we're here together doesn't mean this has
to happen."

"I know." Megan nodded, unable to take her eyes away
from his body.

Sawyer reached down and put a finger under Megan's
chin so she was forced to look in his eyes. "Are you sure?"

"I don't know that I've ever been so sure of anything."
She meant it.

Sawyer snatched the towel out of her hands and quickly
dried his back and legs, but didn't do a very good job of it.

"I think you're still pretty wet," Megan whispered hus-
kily, watching him.

"I don't care." Sawyer echoed his words from earlier.

He threw the towel to the ground and pulled her to him.
They both let out a sigh as their naked bodies touched each
other. Finally.

"Damn, you're beautiful." Sawyer muttered.

Megan reached up and wound her arms around Sawyer's
neck, pulling his lips down to hers for a kiss. She couldn't
be without him for one more second. This time she was
the aggressor, her tongue invading his mouth, teasing him.

Sawyer moaned. He reached down and grabbed her by
the back of the thighs and hiked her legs around his waist,
wrapping his arms under her hips. Megan snaked her arms
more securely around his neck. They both moaned as the
contact brought her breasts against his chest.

Sawyer walked—Megan draped around him—to the
bed, their mouths never separating from their kiss. Then

Megan lost herself in the passion as Sawyer laid her down on the bed and reminded them both of why they were so lucky to be alive.

Chapter Nineteen

The next morning Sawyer stretched out in the bed. Alone. That wasn't how he really wanted it, but he could see Megan through the door of the adjoining room already hard at work on the countermeasure. She was humming as she moved back and forth around the table he had pulled to the middle of the room. Sawyer smiled. Humming had to be a good sign.

It was all he could do to keep from humming himself. Last night had been nothing short of incredible. When Megan had shown up in that bathroom, all of Sawyer's good intentions about letting her rest had completely flown out the window.

And thank heavens for that.

Sawyer was no monk. He'd certainly enjoyed the company of women throughout the years, although not nearly as many as his confirmed-bachelor reputation might suggest. But there was something about that tiny scientist with her giant brain—it had been reinstated from huge back to giant, since she had the good sense to come back into the shower last night—working so steadily in the next room that had Sawyer feeling things he never had before.

Which scared the hell out of him and felt absolutely perfect at the same time.

Sawyer threw the covers off, since he was so warm. The

heater in Megan's workroom must've been on full blast. Of course, she was keeping it that warm so she could work in just his T-shirt.

And that thought—despite the fact that she hadn't been out of his arms all night long, and that neither of them had gotten much sleep—almost had him in the workroom dragging her back to the bed.

But Sawyer knew Megan needed to work. What she was doing now was more important than Sawyer's personal desires.

But he was still tempted. Even knowing she would immediately delve into phrases like *symmetric ciphers* and *source codes* and a bunch of other stuff he didn't understand. Sawyer shook his head, grinning.

Sawyer swung his legs over the side of the bed and got up. He put on his clothes, then made coffee and ate a breakfast of fruit and cereal from the groceries Evan had left. He knew how Megan took her coffee after all these days of working with her, and brought it, along with some food, to the other room. She didn't even look up when he walked through the door.

He set the coffee cup on the table next to her and stood there. Still nothing. It was almost a blow to his ego until he realized she wasn't ignoring him. There could probably be a nuclear holocaust around her and she wouldn't notice.

"Hi," he finally said. Nothing. Her glasses were perched on her nose; she was holding some sort of hand scanner over a circuit board with one arm and typing one-handed into a keyboard with the other. Still humming.

Sawyer finally reached down and cupped her chin, forcing her to look up toward him. He could actually see the exact moment she recognized it was him touching her. Annoyance in her brown eyes melted away to something much more soft. And beautiful.

"Hi," Sawyer said again. "I brought you some coffee and breakfast."

"Thanks," she murmured, taking her glasses off. "I was working."

"I noticed." Sawyer reached down and kissed her. "I don't want to interrupt you, but I wanted to make sure you had something eat."

"Yeah, I sometimes forget when I'm in the middle of a project."

Sawyer looked around. Items were meticulously laid out all over the mattress, where Megan had torn off all the blankets and sheets. Sawyer had no doubt Megan knew the exact location of every item in this room, could find each element blindfolded if she had to.

"You eat this, and get back to it. I'm going to check in with Juliet." He bent down and kissed her, but pulled away before temptation to deepen the kiss could overwhelm either of them. "Nice work outfit by the way. You should try wearing that to the office sometime."

Sawyer laughed as color flooded Megan's cheeks. He kissed the top of her head, then walked into the other room, still chuckling.

Sawyer found one of the cheap no-plan mobile phones he and Megan had bought at the supercenter the day before. Since Sawyer's regular phone had disintegrated along with everything else in the explosion yesterday, he needed something that could keep him in basic communication with Juliet and Evan. He'd gotten a phone for him and one for Megan.

Sawyer dialed a prearranged number. It was neither Juliet's nor Evan's cell phones, just in case someone was listening in on their ends.

"Damn it, Sawyer, you should've checked in last night." Sawyer rolled his eyes at the lack of traditional greeting from his sister.

"I sent the text saying we were out."

"A one-word text lets me know you're alive and is completely acceptable under many circumstances. But you've now been at that motel for more than eight hours."

"Aw, c'mon, Jules—"

"If I pulled something like that, you'd throw a fit. You know it. So don't try your charming act on me."

His sister was right. If she had checked in with only one word, Sawyer would've been worried. But that was because of what happened to her the last time she was in the field. Sawyer didn't want to bring that up.

"You're right, sis. I'm sorry. I should've provided an update once we were secure in the motel."

"Fine. Don't do it again."

"So what's happening at Omega? Anything suspicious?"

"Sawyer, it's the craziest thing. I'm filtering through every system I can, trying to see who might be logging in any suspicious activity. But I'm not finding anything."

"What about me reporting in, then the building blowing up? Does everyone believe I'm dead?"

"Well, that's the thing. When I looked up the handler's computer file for your case, the *original* safe-house location was back in the system. And the last transmission logged is from you, notification that you had made it to the safe house and were planning to stay there for the next few days."

"That's what I said. But I was referring to the second safe house, the one that is now mostly a pile of ash."

"I know. But according to the log-in report, there was never a second safe house mentioned."

"So if our bodies had shown up dead at the second safe house?"

"Nobody at Omega would've had any idea how you got there." They both paused. "It gets worse, Sawyer."

Sawyer rubbed a hand over his face. "Great."

"I've only got reasonable computer-hacking skills, and

whoever is changing all this in the Omega system is way out of my league."

"Does that mean the mole is some computer nerd within Omega?"

"I think it might not be a mole inside Omega at all, Sawyer."

"What?" Sawyer definitely wasn't expecting that.

"Based on how the IP addresses are being bounced around and log-ins are being used, I think it may be someone *outside* Omega completely. Someone hacking a limited part of our system."

"Why would someone just hack a limited part of the system?"

"Anything going too deep would set off all sorts of alarms and red flags. But just getting in, making some small changes and getting back out? If I hadn't been specifically looking for it, I never would've seen it."

"Damn it, Jules. What the hell does this mean?"

There was a pause on the other end. "Sawyer, I have to ask you some questions about Megan. Questions you might not like. Can she hear you?"

Sawyer looked into the other room, where Megan was once again bent over the desk hard at work on the countermeasure.

"She's working in the adjoining room. Not listening to me at all."

"No offense, Sawyer, but are you sure? She's *Dr.* Zane Megan Fuller. Two degrees from MIT. Her IQ is twice ours. Is it possible that she's doing one thing, but also aware of your conversation?"

Sawyer shook his head. He did not like the direction this conversation was going. Especially not after last night. "Just hang on a second," he told Juliet.

Sawyer walked over to the doorway between the two

rooms. He noticed that Megan still hadn't eaten her breakfast, although the coffee was already finished.

"Hey, I'm going to close this door. I'm talking with Juliet and don't want to disturb you."

Megan held up a hand in acknowledgment, but didn't look up from what she was doing or actually respond. But honestly, Sawyer hadn't expected her to. He closed the door between them, grabbed the phone from the bed, then walked into the bathroom and shut that door for good measure.

"All right, Juliet, now I'm sure Megan can't hear me. What the hell are you trying to imply?"

"Look, all I'm asking is for you to keep an open mind."

"Spit it out, Jules."

"I know what changes have been made to the system, so I know what I'm looking for. Some of the suspicious changes are coming from an untraceable IP address, which is to be expected."

"But?" Sawyer prompted.

"But some of the changes are coming from *your* Omega log-in ID, Sawyer, from *your* phone. For anyone who searches deep enough, it looks like you are the one who made the changes in the system."

"But I didn't do anything like that. I'm not even sure I would know how to."

"I know that, baby brother. But there has been someone with you this whole time who very definitely does know how to."

Megan.

"It's not her, Jules. I'm positive about that. It's someone else—whoever the mole is at Cyberdyne."

"I know you don't want to believe it, Sawyer, and I don't blame you. But the last change in the system, erasing the second safe house and reentering the first? That came from your phone's log-in ID. *After* you and Megan had broken out of Cyberdyne."

Sawyer muttered a foul expletive under his breath. It was one thing for his phone to be used while they were still at Cyberdyne. Sawyer didn't want to think it had been taken from him without his knowledge, but it was possible.

But since they'd left Cyberdyne? No one had been in possession of his phone except him. Although Sawyer had to admit there had been minutes where Megan would've had unrestricted access, also. And if the Omega system changes had come from his phone…

Sawyer slammed a fist against the wall. Damn it, had Megan been completely fooling him this entire time? Had last night just been part of the plan to get closer to him?

If so, she'd certainly done that.

"Sawyer…" It was Juliet. Sawyer had completely forgotten he was on the line with her.

"I'll call you back." He hung up without saying anything further.

Sawyer walked out of the bathroom and opened the adjoining door to the rooms and stood in the doorway. As usual, Megan didn't even look up from where she was working and paid no attention to Sawyer whatsoever.

Sawyer tried to relax the tension flowing through his jaw and shoulders. Megan wasn't doing anything suspicious. The opposite, in fact. Hard at work—as she had been for hours—on what he had asked her to do: finish the countermeasure.

As she leaned over the table to reach for something she needed, Sawyer watched as the hem of his T-shirt slid up, giving him a tantalizing glimpse of her upper thigh and the rounded curve of her buttock.

His body instantly responded, memories of last night flooding through him. Evidently his body didn't care if Megan was guilty or not. But damn it, Sawyer refused to believe she was guilty. The hours he had spent with her had shown him who she was. She was brilliant, quirky and often awkward. But she was also kind and patient when others couldn't keep up with what she was saying—which was a lot of the time.

Sawyer had seen her face when her apartment had been robbed and last night when she was so exhausted she didn't even know where she was—nobody outside Broadway was that good of an actress.

And damn it, she came back for him last night in that building. There was no way she could've known how close that bomb was to detonating. Not to mention, if her entire MO had been to kill him, then that would've been the easiest place to do it.

No, his gut—and he'd been trusting it too long to stop now—told him Megan was innocent. Whatever the circumstances were regarding the hacks at Omega, Megan wasn't the one doing it. There had to be some other explanation.

Sawyer couldn't be without her a second longer. He strode over to the table, took what was in her hand and laid it down as gently as he could. He scooped her off her feet, noticing the surprised look on her face as he kissed her almost brutally. He carried her into the bedroom, removing clothes from both of them as he went.

His lovemaking, unlike last night, was unceremonious and almost desperate. Sawyer used it as a weapon to cut away at the accusation that Megan was the traitor.

Because that would mean Sawyer had already lost her forever. A panic unlike any he'd ever known crawled through his gut at the thought. Sawyer pushed those overwhelming feelings away and concentrated on losing himself inside the sweet softness of Megan.

Chapter Twenty

Megan lay sprawled on the bed, unable to will any of her muscles to move. What exactly had that been about? She would've thought that after last night they had gotten all of that lovemaking stuff out of their system.

Evidently not.

But this had been something different. And while Megan had enjoyed every second of it, it was almost as though it had been tinged with desperation. And of all the adjectives she'd use to describe Sawyer—sexy, charming, personable—*desperate* did not make it anywhere on that list.

"This sort of behavior," Megan said, waving her arm around at the bed from where she lay on the pillow next to Sawyer, "is not helping me get the countermeasure completed."

Megan expected some lighthearted or even sarcastic remark from Sawyer. But instead he rolled over so he was lying completely on top of her, face just inches from hers, his weight propped on his elbows.

"You are trying your best to complete the countermeasure, right, Megan?"

Megan wasn't really sure what he meant by the question. Was he making some sort of joke she didn't understand? She wasn't particularly skilled at bedroom talk. "Well, not right at this second I'm not." She smiled at Sawyer, but it faded as he continued to just stare at her intensely.

"Sawyer, what's going on?"

Megan could see Sawyer clench and unclench his jaw, and he seemed to struggle for words. She reached her hands up from between them and cupped his cheeks. "Just tell me. Has something else bad happened?"

Megan didn't think there was anything bad left to happen.

Sawyer still hesitated. "Megan," he finally said. "I need you to be totally honest with me. I will do everything I can to help you, but you've got to be honest with me."

Megan had no idea what he was talking about. "Honest about what?"

"Since we left Cyberdyne, and even before, have you used my phone?"

"The one that you left in the safe house that blew up?"

"Yes? Did you use it at all?"

"No." Megan frowned. His questions did not clarify the matter at all. "I had my own phone. Why would I use yours? Plus we thought someone might be using yours to spy on us. Double reason not to use it."

Sawyer's brows were furrowed together. "For texts, Megan? To send any information? To log in to any systems that my phone would have access to?"

And there it was, the real question he had wanted to ask. *Had she used his phone to log in somewhere she shouldn't have been?*

Megan had always considered her intellect a blessing and a privilege. Her ability to look at random pieces of a problem—even with some pieces missing—and figure out how they worked together as a whole was her gift.

But she very much wished she didn't have that ability right now. She was able to understand what Sawyer was hinting at without him having to say the words outright.

Sawyer thought she was the traitor. That she had used his phone to access Omega's system and plant false info.

"Get off me. Right now." Megan said it softly, slowly.

"Meg—"

"Right now!" This time her voice was much louder, barely lower than a yell.

Sawyer rolled to the side and Megan flew off the bed, bringing the sheet with her and wrapping it around herself.

"You think *I'm* the traitor?" Megan whispered, backing away from the bed.

"Megan—"

"And you just did *that*—" she gestured to the bed "—with me, thinking I was a traitor?"

"No." Sawyer shook his head, sliding toward her. Megan took a step back. If he touched her now she would shatter into a million pieces. "No, I knew you weren't. Megan, I knew you weren't. That's why I made love with you again."

Megan just clutched the sheet tighter to herself. "Then why would you ask me those questions, Sawyer?"

Sawyer reached over and pulled on his jeans. He sat on the edge of the bed and put his head in his hands. Megan felt as if cold was permeating her entire body.

"Megan, Juliet told me that there's not a mole inside Omega at all. The system has been hacked and that's how the information was given to me about the false safe house. And it looks like my phone has been used to access info in the Omega system since you and I broke out of Cyberdyne."

"And you and I were the only ones to have access to your phone during that time." Megan whispered the obvious statement.

"Yes." Sawyer looked up from his hands and stood up. Megan took another step backward.

"But even when Juliet told me that," Sawyer continued, "I knew it wasn't you. I knew there had to be something else. Some other way my phone was being used."

"Then why ask me that, Sawyer? Why?" Her voice broke on the last word.

"Megan, you're so much smarter than me. Than all of us. If you had done something stupid, or under duress, or because you were scared, I just wanted to give you the chance to tell me. To let you know that I would help you, protect you in any way I could."

The tears Megan couldn't keep back finally fell. He hadn't really believed she was innocent. He had made love to her thinking she was a liar and a traitor.

"Megan." Sawyer took another step toward her, but stopped when she held out an arm in front of her. "I handled it wrong. I'm sorry. I should've told you what Juliet said about the phone and together we would have figured out how it could've happened and what it all meant."

Megan nodded, but didn't say anything. Yes, that was how he should've handled it.

She needed to be away from him. She felt as if her heart was breaking, which was silly because they'd only spent one night together. But she needed to be alone where she wouldn't feel so exposed and vulnerable.

Megan knew she really couldn't blame Sawyer for reacting to the news about the phone hack like a cop. That was what he was. The same way she tended to overanalyze everything because she was a scientist. That was what she was.

But right now she was simply a woman who had been accused of something terrible by the man she had just given herself to so completely mere hours—*minutes*—before.

So, yes, her brain could understand Sawyer's questions and his need for them. But her heart was having a much more difficult time.

SAWYER WOULD GIVE everything he owned to never see that look on Megan's face again. She had been so strong through everything—harm to her body, seeing her possessions destroyed, losing her job—and now Sawyer's heart broke as he watched the tears flood out of her eyes and onto her cheeks. She looked at him as if he had just killed something precious.

And Sawyer was desperately afraid he had.

"I'm going to get dressed and get back to work," Megan whispered.

"Megan—" Sawyer reached for her wanting to do something, *anything*, to take away that look in her eyes.

"No," she told him, taking another step away. "You're law enforcement. I get it. But right now, I just need you not to touch me." She turned and fled into the bathroom. Moments later Sawyer heard the shower running.

Sawyer sat back down on the bed. How had he screwed this up to such a monumental degree? His gut had told him Megan didn't do this. He should've just trusted that and left it alone. Or talked to her about all the possibilities. God knew with her giant brain she could come up with some ideas about what could have happened that he'd never even considered.

Instead he had taken her to bed and then promptly accused her of treason. Just what a woman always wanted.

Sawyer got dressed. He should be thankful Megan hadn't told him to go to hell and stormed out of here refusing to finish the countermeasure after the way he had just behaved.

But she didn't. And she was going back to work on it. Because that was just the type of person she was.

Sawyer grimaced. He had to make this right with her. But damned if he knew how.

He decided to call Juliet back while Megan was in the shower.

"As of right now, we work based on the assumption that Megan Fuller did not use my phone and log-in ID to make any of the hacks at Omega," Sawyer told Juliet without greeting.

"Sawyer—"

"No, Juliet. She didn't do it. It happened some other way. We have to figure out what that is."

"Okay."

"Okay?" Sawyer hadn't thought it would be that easy to convince his sister.

"Sawyer, you're there with her. I'm not. If you say you know she didn't do it, then I believe you. I'll start running other possibilities."

"Thanks, Jules."

"I'll take care of things on this end. You guys just get the countermeasure finished."

"We will."

"And, Sawyer, you two be careful. There are still too many unknowns in this situation for my peace of mind."

Megan was coming out of the shower as Sawyer hung up with Juliet. She was wrapped in a towel.

"I need my clothes." Megan grabbed her bag and went back into the bathroom without another word. When she exited a few minutes later, she was fully dressed in her own clothes.

Sawyer guessed she probably wouldn't be wearing just his shirt anytime soon.

"Megan, I'm sorry—"

"Look, Sawyer, like I said, I can't blame you for assuming the worst. That's your job, I guess." She threw the bag down and crossed to the doorway of the other room. "But right now, I don't want to talk about it. I don't know if I'm ever going to want to talk about."

Every word was a dagger to Sawyer's heart. But he couldn't blame her.

"Right now," she continued, "I just want to work. That's what I'm best at and probably what I should stick to." She walked into the other room, turned down the blasting heat and began working.

There were so many things Sawyer wanted to say to Megan, but he didn't allow himself to do so. Because ultimately she was right: their personal problems were secondary to getting the countermeasure finished. That had to take priority.

Sawyer hoped he would have a chance to apologize— and that she would listen—once the mission was completed.

Chapter Twenty-One

Sawyer watched Megan work tirelessly for the next day and a half. She ate only when Sawyer reminded her to, and slept only once, at her desk. Sawyer tried to carry her to the bed when she slept, but she immediately awoke and wanted to get back to work.

She didn't talk to him at all, except to politely thank him for any food or assistance he brought her. She just worked. And worked and worked.

Her ability to concentrate and figure out all the complex parts of the countermeasure would've been quite impressive to Sawyer if he could get over the heavy feeling in the pit of his stomach. He had screwed up so badly. The more he thought about it, the more he realized how much he had hurt Megan by his accusation. Especially the timing of it.

If he could reach his own ass, he would kick it. Multiple times.

There was nothing he could do now but not interrupt her and allow her to finish the countermeasure. Then he'd get it to Omega and spend however long it took to make Megan accept his apology. But until then all he could do was sit here and wish he had handled the whole situation better. Him, the person Omega sent in when they needed someone with finesse with people. Well, finesse had been nowhere to be seen this time.

Sawyer stood up from the table where he'd sat for the past few hours. It was dinnertime and he was tired of eating microwaved junk. They needed some real, fresh food. And Sawyer needed a chance to get out of this room where he was constantly surrounded by his mistakes. Not to mention Sawyer wanted to call Juliet again—totally out of Megan's earshot—to see if any progress had been made.

Sawyer walked into the other room, where Megan worked. He could see exhaustion in her features and marveled at how she just pushed it aside. He walked over to stand behind her and gently began rubbing her shoulders.

For just a moment Megan sighed and relaxed into his hands. She tilted her head so her cheek rested against one of his hands that massaged her. But then Sawyer felt awareness—and tension—creep back into her form. Soon she was totally stiff, so Sawyer stopped and removed his hands.

"Thank you," she said in that polite tone he was coming to detest.

"How are things going here? Is there anything I can do to help?" Sawyer had made the offer more than once over the past few hours. He maybe didn't have a giant brain, but he had a pretty steady pair of hands.

"I'm close, Sawyer. Just a couple more hours, I think. But fatigue is pulling at me. Making me slower."

"Why don't you lie down for a few minutes?" He saw Megan's panicked glance at the bed and sighed. "Not with me. I'm going out to get us some fresh food. You can rest, refresh your brain, for just a few minutes while I'm gone."

Megan rubbed a weary hand over her face, removing her glasses. "That's probably a good idea."

Sawyer walked with her over to the bed. She lay down and he pulled the covers over her. He got the second phone they had picked up at the store and placed it on the nightstand next to her.

"If you need anything, use this phone, not the motel phone. Speed dial one is my phone, two is my sister, Juliet. But I should be back in just a few minutes. I'll leave you the car in case you need it."

Megan nodded, her big brown eyes looking up at him. Sawyer couldn't help it—he had to touch her. He brushed some of Megan's unruly hair out of her face. She didn't flinch away. That was at least a start.

He reached down and kissed her, but pulled back before either of them had to choose whether to really engage in the kiss or not. But she didn't turn away from him. Another start.

"Sawyer..." Megan whispered hesitantly.

Sawyer wasn't sure if she was going to say something good or bad. Either way it didn't need to be said now.

"Sleep," he told her. "We can talk later."

She brought her hand out from under the covers and grabbed his as he was standing. "Be careful. Hurry back."

Sawyer nodded and Megan let his hand go, snuggling herself back into the blankets. Sawyer wished he could be the one there keeping her warm. But at least she was talking to him. It was a start.

SAWYER WAS WALKING back from the deli where he'd bought sandwiches and salads thirty minutes later when he realized he was being followed. He'd almost missed it, but someone had turned a little too sharply away from Sawyer when he'd left the deli. That small movement had caught his attention.

Sawyer kept walking, at a faster-than-casual pace. But he had circled around so he was leading them away from the motel. Sawyer glanced around as he walked. As far as he could tell, there were three people following him. Make that four.

Sawyer didn't know how DS-13 had found them—something he'd missed at the safe house?—but at this moment he didn't care. The most important thing right now was to keep them away from Megan. Obviously, DS-13 didn't know about the motel or they would've been there already.

Sawyer tried cutting down a different road, speeding up as he turned a corner, attempting to lose his followers. But with four of them there wasn't much use. Realizing Sawyer knew they were following him, and therefore wasn't unwittingly going to lead them to Megan and the counter-measure, they had dropped all pretense of secrecy.

Now they just wanted to capture Sawyer.

Sawyer ducked inside a small restaurant, a mom-and-pop place busy with Asheville locals coming out for a meal. Sawyer scanned the room as he walked seemingly casually through the restaurant. An older couple, just removing their jackets and sitting down at a table, provided him with what he was looking for.

Sawyer set the deli bags down on a recently vacated table and grabbed a glass of water. He made his way toward the older couple. As he neared them, he tripped, spilling the water on their table.

"Oh my goodness, I'm so sorry," Sawyer gushed to them. "I'm so clumsy." He grabbed paper napkins from the dispenser on the table and began wiping up the mess.

"It's only water, young man," the older woman told him. "Don't you worry about it."

Sawyer slid closer to the man and continued to mop up the water. "It's my first day working here. Why don't you move to this table right over here and I'll get this table cleaned up?"

Sawyer removed the couple's jackets from their chairs—slipping the man's car keys out of the pocket while he did so—and moved them to a new table. He apologized for the spill again and then quickly made his way toward the back of the restaurant.

Reaching the couple's car would be his best chance to

get away from the DS-13 men following him. There was no way Sawyer could escape them on foot.

Sawyer went out the back kitchen door, ignoring startled looks from employees, and circled back to the parking lot. He pushed the lock button on the vehicle's keyless-entry remote, knowing the sound would draw attention, but it was the only way to know which car was the couple's.

He heard the honk and made his way toward the area, ducking between other cars as he saw two of the DS-13 men come out the kitchen door of the restaurant. Sawyer had no idea where the other two men were, but they were around here somewhere.

This was going to be close.

Sawyer beeped the horn again. There. A silver Toyota just a few yards away. Perfect. Sawyer made a dash for it, looking over his shoulder. The two by the back door saw him and were running, but as long as they were planning to take him alive, they would be too far away to catch him.

Sawyer unlocked the car as he ran to it. He threw the driver's side door open and dived in, glancing out the passenger side at the two men running toward him. Sawyer was starting the ignition and attempting to lock the door when the driver's side door opened and a gun was pressed to his temple.

"I'm going to need you to step out of your car, Agent Branson."

Damn it, the other two men had circled around the other way. Sawyer hadn't seen them, but they had obviously seen him. And now they had him. Sawyer turned off the car.

"Slowly," the man with the gun told Sawyer. "And just in case you're thinking of making any big scene, we will kill any bystander who comes over here to see what is going on."

Sawyer stepped out of the car and got a good look at the assailant. This was the same hooded guy who had broken into Megan's apartment and put a knife to her throat and sliced Sawyer's arm.

"You look a little more proper without the hoodie," Sawyer told the man as Hoodie reached over and pulled Sawyer's sidearm out of the holster inside his jacket.

Hoodie nodded and smirked at him. "How's the arm?"

Sawyer walked, flanked by the four men, farther back behind the restaurant, down an alley near a Dumpster. He didn't make any attempt to get away. Sawyer couldn't risk it; he had to take them at their word that they would kill bystanders.

As soon as they were out of direct vision of other people, they stopped. Two of the men grabbed Sawyer by each arm in case he was inclined to run.

"We're going to need you to tell us where Dr. Fuller and the stuff she took from Cyberdyne are," Hoodie, obviously the leader of this group by the way they kept looking to him for instruction, said.

"She took the stuff and split, man. I haven't seen her in days." Sawyer gave him a friendly grin.

Hoodie nodded to one of the other men holding Sawyer's arm. Before Sawyer could even brace for it, he punched Sawyer in the gut.

Sawyer doubled over, coughing, only part of it for show. But the longer he could stretch things out here, the safer Megan would be.

"Want to try that again, Agent Branson? We know you made it out of the safe house with her, but then we lost you. Where is she?"

"Look, take it easy. I'm not trying to piss you off, but she's gone, man. Once we figured out the safe house was a trap, the FBI took her into protective custody." Sawyer damn well wished that really *was* what had happened right now.

"You better hope that's not the case, Agent Branson, or

you won't be much use to my boss. That probably won't bode well for you."

Sawyer would take his chances with the DS-13 boss. He shrugged. "It is what it is, man. She's gone."

That got him another punch, this time in the face. Sawyer spit out blood from where his cheek had ground into his teeth.

"Then why are you still here, smart guy? Where is Dr. Fuller?" Another punch in the face.

Sawyer was momentarily saved when Hoodie received a phone call. He turned away—obviously to speak to someone important. Sawyer knew this would be his only chance. If he didn't get out now, torture and death at the hands of DS-13 most certainly would be his fate.

Not to mention leaving Megan unprotected and exposed.

Sawyer kept his body slumped over for a moment—not difficult considering the punches he'd already taken. But then he burst forward into action, jerking the gun away from one of the men holding him. Elbowing the other man, the one who had hit him, in the jaw on the way to standing fully upright was Sawyer's pleasure.

Their skirmish drew the attention of the fourth man, the lookout a few feet away. He rushed over, giving Sawyer three men to deal with. Sawyer punched the first man in the jaw, then sent him flying with a kick. But the other two were already on him. One grabbed Sawyer in a bear hug, forcing Sawyer to head-butt him to get free. Sawyer heard the man howl in pain and figured he'd just broken his nose.

Sawyer turned to face the third man. He didn't want to waste time fighting him, just wanted to get past him so he could escape while the other two were still on the ground and the leader was occupied on the phone.

But then everything turned gray as a blow came to the back of his head. Sawyer fought to hold on to consciousness as he fell to his knees. "My men are idiots, Agent Branson."

The leader was bouncing his pistol casually in his hand—obviously what he had just used to hit Sawyer with. "I'd like to get rid of you right now, but evidently we're going to need your cooperation to get Dr. Fuller and the counter-measure she's working on."

Then he punched Sawyer in the jaw, and holding on to consciousness wasn't an option.

Chapter Twenty-Two

Sawyer woke up tied to a chair. Without giving away that he was conscious, he tried to take stock of the situation. Six men in the room, four he recognized from the alley. One behind him that he couldn't really see. But the last one…

Fred McNeil. The crooked FBI agent. The one who had given DS-13 Ghost Shell in the first place and had almost killed his brother a few weeks ago. And based on listening to their conversations for a few minutes, it looked as though McNeil was in charge.

The building itself seemed to be some sort of trailer. Glancing as inconspicuously as possible out the window, it looked as if they were in a junkyard. That did not bode well. Too many places where a body could be dumped and never found.

Sawyer had no idea how long he'd been out or how far they were from the motel.

"Looks like Sleeping Beauty is finally waking up." It was McNeil. "Agent Branson, we haven't had the pleasure of meeting, although I did meet your brother."

"Yeah, McNeil. I know who you are." Sawyer had to spit some blood out of his mouth so he could continue. "I can't say it's a pleasure, though."

McNeil chuckled in a way that made Sawyer's skin crawl. "You look like your brother. Cam Cameron. God,

I should've known something wasn't right when they told me that was his name. No real person would have a name like Cam Cameron. It had to be someone working undercover." McNeil shook his head. "Your brother certainly took down a large chunk of DS-13. And cost me a lot of money."

"Cameron's been a problem child since birth." Sawyer shifted in the chair, testing the bonds on his wrists tied behind him. Unfortunately, there wasn't any give in the thin cords. "I'd be happy to deliver him to you if you want to let me go."

McNeil came over and stood right in front of Sawyer. "Tempting, but I think not. You all actually did me a favor when you got rid of Mr. Smith. One less person taking a chunk of the money."

Somehow Sawyer didn't think the former head of DS-13 would agree, but didn't mention it.

"But you also took Ghost Shell. Frustrating." McNeil sighed dramatically. "But at least I had the other Ghost Shell version, although it wasn't quite as operational. Fortunately, we got someone to help us overcome that problem."

"Oh yeah, who's that?"

"I wanted the best to help us, and believe me, I scoped out Dr. Fuller for that role. But she wasn't interested. Cold fish, that one."

Sawyer barely refrained from smirking. He thought of his night spent with Megan. To call her a cold fish was ridiculous. She just had the good sense not to get involved with the likes of Fred McNeil. Sawyer shrugged. No point antagonizing someone who already had you tied to a chair and planned to do you bodily harm. "Women. Whatcha gonna do?"

"See, I already like you better than your brother. So much more reasonable. But I found someone better than Megan, actually months ago when I first was at Cyberdyne. Someone able to complete our version of Ghost Shell and who has excellent hacking skills—with cloned phones." McNeil crouched down in front of Sawyer. "Very helpful for when we needed to know where you were."

There it was, verbal proof that Megan wasn't the traitor.

Sawyer thought he might feel some tiny measure of relief upon hearing the news, convincing that last little part of him of her innocence. But no, in his heart he had already been 100 percent convinced. He didn't need any jackass like McNeil announcing Megan's innocence to know it was true.

"So we got the next best thing. You remember Jonathan Bushman, Dr. Fuller's assistant?"

Bushman stepped up from behind Sawyer. "You." Sawyer all but spat the word. "She trusted you."

Jonathan scoffed, "The esteemed Dr. Fuller didn't trust me. She always thought I wasn't smart enough to work with her on the truly important projects. She's been that way for years. Always wanting to work alone because she thinks she's so ridiculously brilliant."

How could Sawyer have missed the disdain Jonathan had for Megan? Sawyer had been too busy looking for the traitor in the faces of other Cyberdyne employees and missed what was right under his nose.

"It was you, not Trish," Sawyer said.

Bushman rolled his eyes. "Trish was a pawn to divert your attention from me. She doesn't know anything about this. Sorry you were too stupid to figure that out."

Sawyer wished that for just ten seconds his hands could be untied so he could punch Jonathan in his whiny face.

"And now Megan's going to get what's coming to her," Bushman continued. "Because after the stunt she pulled at Cyberdyne, nobody's ever going to hire her in the computer R & D field again. I'll finally get my shot at being director."

Sawyer shook his head. If DS-13 had their way, Megan wouldn't work again in the R & D field because she'd be dead. They weren't going to let her—or Sawyer—out of here alive once they had what they wanted.

"Plus, I'll have a little lucrative work on the side, provided by McNeil," Jonathan continued. "Best of both worlds, and no Megan around to lord her brilliance over all of us."

Sawyer shook his head as Jonathan walked away. If that was what Jonathan really thought of Megan, then he was obviously delusional. Arguing with him wouldn't help.

"So with the help of Mr. Bushman here, we have the new Ghost Shell ready to be sold," McNeil continued. "But unfortunately, word of the countermeasure Dr. Fuller is working on has already leaked out. That news is making Ghost Shell less potentially profitable than I had hoped. So I'm going to need the countermeasure."

"Yeah." Sawyer dragged the word out. "I don't have it."

"I'm aware of that, Branson. But Dr. Fuller does. Where is she?"

"In protective custody, probably somewhere in Virginia. Or maybe Oklahoma."

Sawyer wasn't prepared for the fist that hit him on the jaw. His head flew to the side. He couldn't keep from groaning and had to spit blood again.

McNeil stood up, rubbing his fist. "I hope that's not the case, for your sake." He held out his hand and Hoodie brought over a phone.

Sawyer's phone.

"You really should be more careful with your phones, Agent Branson. First you allowed your Omega phone to be cloned by Jonathan. Then he could access Omega's system—limited access, but enough to do harm. And now you've lost this one."

McNeil came and stood in front of Sawyer again. "Looks like a pretty cheap phone. You probably won't be too sad to lose this one. Only a couple of numbers stored. Let's try them."

Sawyer struggled against the ties that bound him, but could not get loose in any way.

McNeil laughed. "Oh, so now I seem to have your attention. Care to revise your statement about the location of Dr. Fuller?"

"Screw you, McNeil. She's somewhere you're never going to be able to get to her."

"Why don't we test that theory, Branson? Let's give the lovely Dr. Fuller a call, shall we? We'll put it on speaker to make it more fun."

Sawyer watched helplessly as McNeil began to dial the number to Megan's phone.

AFTER SAWYER LEFT, Megan had lain in the bed expecting sleep to overtake her, but it hadn't. She just couldn't get her brain to shut down. Too much thinking about the countermeasure and, if she was honest, about Sawyer.

Megan was still hurt that he would accuse her of being a traitor while lying next to her naked in the bed. But when she thought through the actual conversation they'd had, Megan realized Sawyer had been stretching himself far outside his law-enforcement comfort zone.

He had thought there was a possibility she had gotten herself in trouble and had been offering to help.

Okay, yeah, he'd had terrible timing in the offering of his assistance, but at least he'd been willing to listen to her side of the story, rather than just assume the worst. For a man who fought for justice so unflinchingly, that had to mean something.

So when she really thought about it, Megan realized Sawyer was trying to show he cared.

Megan still wasn't ready to just forgive and forget, but neither was she going to continue to consider it the crime of the century. Sawyer was a man. He'd said something stupid at the wrong time. He wasn't the first or the last man to do so.

Plus, now that Megan was almost finished with the countermeasure, they had only a few days left before Sawyer headed back to Omega Sector headquarters. Megan didn't want to spend that time fighting. She'd have plenty of time to be alone when she was attempting to put her life—in all of its many broken pieces—back together after Sawyer was gone.

And Sawyer would be gone; Megan was sure of that. He was not the serious-commitment type of guy. She had known that going into all of this, so she wasn't going to regret it now.

Megan got out of the bed. Sleep was nowhere to be found, so she may as well keep working. She didn't know how long Sawyer would be gone.

She was so lost in her work a little while later that it took three or four rings for Megan to realize the phone Sawyer had bought for her was ringing. She stood and rushed to the table to get it. It must be Sawyer; he was the only one with the number.

"Good to finally hear from you, stranger." Megan laughed into the phone, hoping her joking tone would help Sawyer know she wasn't so mad anymore.

But silence met her.

"Sawyer?" Megan was much more hesitant. Was he mad at her now?

"Megan, don't listen to them—" Sawyer's words were cut off in a whoosh of breath.

"Sawyer?" What was happening? "Are you all right? Sawyer?" Megan was panicked when he didn't respond.

Then a much louder voice came on the line. "Hello, Dr. Fuller. It's Fred McNeil. Do you remember me?"

Fred McNeil. Yes, Megan definitely remembered him,

and not in any sort of good way. She shuddered just thinking about him. "What do you want?"

"We want you to deliver the countermeasure you've been
working on to us."

"Megan, no—" She heard Sawyer call out again before
his words were cut off, by a blow, Megan was sure. She
flinched.

Megan didn't know what to do. Did she bluff and pretend like she didn't have the countermeasure? Would they
kill Sawyer if she told them that?

Chances were they would kill them both if she just
handed the countermeasure over to them.

"I don't have it anymore." Megan prayed she was saying the right thing. "I handed it over to the FBI. The *real*
FBI this time, McNeil. I can't get it."

"Hmm. That's unfortunate for Agent Branson, Megan.
Let's talk to him about that for a moment."

There was silence for several moments before Megan
heard the sickening crunch of a human bone being broken. She heard Sawyer's deep moan of pain before he silenced himself.

"Sawyer!" Megan sobbed, bile pooling in her stomach.

"Megan, no." Sawyer said it through deep gasps of
breath.

"Now, that's a shame. It looks like Agent Branson's arm
is pretty broken. But don't worry, he still has his other one.
And his legs, and all his fingers and toes. Lots of unbro-
ken bones still left."

Tears poured down Megan's cheeks. What was she supposed to do?

"Fine, McNeil. Just stop, please. I'll bring you the
countermeasure."

"I thought you said the real FBI already has it."

"No, they don't. I have it. I'm in a safe house."

"Megan—" They cut him off again with another blow. Megan couldn't stop the sob that escaped her.

She knew what Sawyer was trying to tell her. McNeil would kill both of them once he had the countermeasure. Sawyer didn't want her to give up her life. But neither was Megan going to allow them to torture Sawyer to death.

"You need to bring me the countermeasure." McNeil provided her with an address just outside Asheville. "Right now."

"Fine, McNeil, but I'm in Charlotte. Omega didn't think the Asheville area was a good place for me to stay after DS-13 blew up the safe house." Megan closed her eyes and prayed this bluff would work. It was the only shot. "It's going to take me a couple of hours to get to you."

"Fine. Two hours. After that, I will break one of Agent Branson's bones per minute."

Megan bit back her sob. "I'll be there."

"And if there is any sign of police or anyone else, I will kill handsome Sawyer here in the most painful way possible."

Megan heard another thud and groan. She thought she might vomit.

"Clock's ticking, Dr. Fuller."

Megan stared at the silent phone in her hand. Her mind kept replaying the sickening crunch of Sawyer's arm breaking.

Megan wasn't sure what to do, but she knew she couldn't do anything alone. Sawyer was right: if she showed up and just turned over the countermeasure, there was nothing to stop McNeil and DS-13 from just killing them outright.

Megan punched the button for the other number stored in her phone: Sawyer's sister, Juliet. But it was a man who answered.

"Sawyer?" the man asked.

"Who is this?" Megan asked. "Where's Juliet?"

"Is this Dr. Fuller? I'm Evan Karcz. We talked briefly on the phone a few days ago. You might remember my foot being firmly planted in my mouth during that conversation."

Yes, Megan did remember Sawyer's friend Evan. "I thought this number was for Juliet."

"She's inside Omega right now, so she had calls from this number forwarded to me. Where's Sawyer?"

Megan felt the sobs bubbling out of her. "They have him."

An ugly expletive burst from Evan. "What? Who?"

"Fred McNeil." Another expletive from Evan upon hearing that news. "Sawyer went out to get us some dinner, but then I got a call from McNeil saying to bring the countermeasure." She gave Evan the address. "I only have two hours."

"Why did they give you that long?"

"I told them I was in Charlotte and couldn't get there before then."

"Smart, Dr. Fuller. You probably just saved Sawyer's life with that bit of quick thinking."

Something tight inside Megan loosened just a little, until she remembered… "Oh, God, Evan, they hurt Sawyer. Broke his arm while I was on the phone with them. Said they would break the rest of his bones—"

"Megan." Evan didn't let her continue. "We're going to get him out."

"How?"

"I'm nearby and you're nearby. McNeil doesn't know that and we're going to use it to our advantage."

"Okay." A plan. Megan knew she needed to focus on a plan in order to keep from panicking. "How?"

"Do you have enough stuff to build something that looks like a fake countermeasure device?"

Megan looked around. She didn't have much. "Maybe. I could probably fool the average person."

"Can you fool McNeil?"

"I think so, yes. But only for a little while."

"Okay, build something quickly, make it seem as legitimate as possible. But, Megan, you need to leave the real countermeasure at the hotel. If something goes wrong, we can't take a chance on McNeil and DS-13 having both Ghost Shell and the countermeasure."

"But—"

"Megan, Sawyer would want it that way. You know that."

Megan sighed. She did know that. But she didn't like it.

"I'm going to get a couple of local law enforcement I know I can trust and head over there. I'm looking up the address McNeil gave you, and it seems like it's a junkyard, which is both good and bad. I will try to get Sawyer out before you even arrive, but if you don't hear from me, go in at the scheduled time."

"And do what?"

"Show them the fake countermeasure. Stall as long as possible. Don't get yourself killed and be ready to run at any moment."

All that sounded a lot easier said than done. "You know I'm not an agent, right, Evan?"

"After all the great things Sawyer's said about you, I have no doubt you'll do fine."

Megan hoped so; all their lives depended on it.

Chapter Twenty-Three

Despite the cold weather, sweat pooled on Sawyer's forehead as he sat in the room. Everything in his body hurt, but his broken arm, now retied to the chair, was the worst.

No, knowing Megan was on her way here to face down McNeil and his cronies, and not being able to get out of this damn chair, was the worst.

The sun had set not long ago and Sawyer knew time was running out. He wasn't sure where McNeil and Bushman were, but they weren't in this room. Only one guy, looking bored and mad not to be part of the action, stood guard here with Sawyer. Which just served to frustrate Sawyer more. He was one measly guard away from being able to save Megan.

Sawyer knew he had only one option, but it was going to hurt. He took a deep breath and began rocking until he tipped over his chair.

Even landing on his uninjured arm, the pain was excruciating, rocketing through his entire body. Sawyer fought to hold on to consciousness.

"What happened? Did you pass out?"

As Sawyer had hoped, the guard came over to see what the commotion was about. Sawyer pretended to be unconscious, then kicked out the guard's knees when he was close enough, causing the man to crumple to the floor. Sawyer then spun—gritting his teeth from the agony in his arm—and kicked the guy as hard as he could in the chin. The guard fell back, unmoving. Sawyer scooted around until he was able to grab his gun.

Sawyer used all his strength to shift his weight, cursing violently as he was able to break off part of the chair. His hands weren't completely free, but at least now he was able to move. Sweat poured down his face as Sawyer took unsteady steps toward the door.

He saw the doorknob turn and jumped to the side, hugging the wall. Sawyer couldn't get a good grip on the gun with his functional arm because of the pieces of the chair he was still tied to. He placed the gun in the hand of his broken arm, praying his fingers would work when he needed to pull the trigger.

The door opened too slowly to be a member of DS-13. Sawyer didn't let his guard down, but didn't attack, either. A man he didn't recognize, dressed in black, entered the room, weapon raised. Sawyer put his gun against the man's temple.

"I really don't want to have to kill you. And my fingers may be a little trigger-happy, so you should definitely not make any sudden movements."

"Agent Branson?"

"Who are you?"

"I'm with Agent Evan Karcz. We're here to help get you out."

A voice came from behind the man. "Sawyer, if you're done messing around, there are some bad guys to get rid of."

Sawyer lowered his weapon. Only Evan would say something that asinine.

The other man with Evan moved into the room to secure the unconscious guard. Evan helped Sawyer get loose from the rest of the chair. "Damn, Sawyer. You look like hell."

"Yeah, thanks." Sawyer grimaced as Evan helped him splint his agonizing arm against his chest. Then Sawyer pushed the pain aside. "Evan, talk to me. Is Megan okay? Please tell me she's not coming here."

"I couldn't stop her, man. It was our best possibility of getting you out. By now, she's already here. I had her leave the countermeasure at the motel and piece together a fake. She felt pretty confident that she'd be able to fool McNeil and buy us some time."

Sawyer cursed under his breath. "It's not just McNeil she has to fool. It's her assistant, Jonathan Bushman. He's the mole who has been working for McNeil and DS-13. She won't be able to trick Bushman for long. Where are they?"

"It looked like McNeil and his men are camped near the main fence. It's a good vantage point for them, junk piles on three sides. No easy way in or out. I left one man there covering everything with a rifle, but he won't be able to take out everyone…"

Before Megan got killed. Evan didn't say it, but Sawyer knew it was the truth. If bullets started flying, Megan would be in the middle of it.

Time to change the plan.

"Evan, grab another chair and tie me to it—they won't recognize it's a different one in the dark. And get rid of the guard. McNeil's men will be coming for me. He'll want me down there to keep her in line. They'll have to untie me and won't be expecting me to have a weapon."

"Sawyer, no offense, man, but are you sure you can even fire a weapon right now? You look like you might keel over any second."

"You guys just get over to where Megan is meeting McNeil. I'll make it. Be ready to move, and take out all of McNeil's men, on my signal."

Sawyer tucked the guard's gun into the waistband of his jeans, under his shirt. Then Evan helped take the splint off

Sawyer's arm and tied him back to the chair. Sawyer took deep breaths to try to keep the pain in check.

"Hang in there, man," Evan told him on the way out the door.

"Evan, Megan's the most important thing. She makes it out of here alive, no matter what. You make sure your men know that."

"Roger that." Evan disappeared into the night.

They were almost too late. Just a few minutes later one of McNeil's men—Hoodie, just Sawyer's luck—stormed into the trailer. He looked around for a moment. "Where the hell is Edwards?"

Sawyer didn't respond, so the man walked over and kicked Sawyer's chair, sending pain radiating throughout his body. His moan of pain didn't have to be faked. "Hey, where is Edwards? The guard."

"I don't know." Sawyer mumbled the words.

"That screwup never knows when to stay put." Hoodie was still cursing as he untied Sawyer and began pulling him out of the trailer. Just as Sawyer suspected, the man didn't retie Sawyer's hands and definitely didn't think to check him for weapons. Given how swollen Sawyer's broken arm was, Sawyer didn't blame him.

But that didn't mean Sawyer wouldn't use the underestimation to his advantage.

MEGAN'S HEART POUNDED as if she was running a sprint. She was driving into this junkyard by herself, taking the word of a man she'd never met—just because he was Sawyer's best friend—that he would protect her somehow.

She was bringing in a useless piece of hardware to pass off as a sophisticated anti-encoding hard drive. A technically savvy ten-year-old would be able to see through it in moments.

The real countermeasure was supposed to be back at the

motel, but it wasn't. It was under the passenger seat. The longer she had waited for Evan's call, the more frantic she had become. When she couldn't wait any longer, and had to leave immediately in order to make it to the junkyard in time, she had made a decision: she would bring the real countermeasure. If the countermeasure could possibly save Sawyer's life, then she was damn sure going to have it as an option. Omega Sector would just have to find some other way of getting it back.

Megan could feel her heart beating again and wondered vaguely if she would have a heart attack and all of this would be for naught anyway. She took some deep breaths to try to get herself under control.

Evan Karcz had told her to stall if she got to this point without word from him. Megan tried not to imagine all the things that could've gone wrong that would've led to him *not* calling. Those thoughts would just get her pulse up in the stratosphere again.

Megan pulled up to where Fred McNeil stood, along with a bunch of his gang, or whatever they were called, and got out of the car.

Stall.

"Dr. Fuller, so nice to see you again," McNeil said.

"Sorry, I can't say the same thing, Mr. McNeil." Megan looked around. "Where's Sawyer?"

Fred McNeil laughed curtly. "Always so abrupt. He's coming. Where is the countermeasure?"

"Right here." Megan held up the fake device. "But you should know that unless I enter a certain code, this device will transmit its blueprints to every law-enforcement agency in the state. New countermeasures can be made within a day."

Megan almost scoffed at the size of her own lie, but managed to refrain.

"She's lying. There's no way it could do that."

Megan's head spun around at the sound. She could not believe what she was hearing. "Jonathan? *You're* the one working for them? Why?"

Jonathan rolled his eyes. "I actually found some people who appreciated my abilities. You certainly never did."

Megan shook her head. "I don't understand. I always appreciated your work."

"Yeah, I could tell that by how you always wanted to work alone. Always thought you were better than everyone else."

"Enough," McNeil called out. "Look, here's Agent Branson joining us right now. A little worse for wear. Sorry about that."

Megan's throat dried up at the sight of Sawyer. His arm—obviously the broken one—was held at a terrible angle against his chest. His face was battered and swollen. Megan couldn't believe he was even able to walk on his own—not that he really was walking; he was almost being dragged by the man with him. The man Megan recognized from the attack at her house.

McNeil grabbed Sawyer and threw him toward Megan. Megan cried out and caught Sawyer the best she could as he stumbled, moaning. He seemed barely conscious. "See? Sawyer is alive. Now give us the countermeasure."

Megan couldn't even figure out how to possibly stall any longer. Evan Karcz better make his move soon.

"Here." Megan held up the fake countermeasure, her other arm around Sawyer. But she knew it wouldn't fool Jonathan, not even for a moment.

"Bushman, check it out."

Jonathan took the drive from Megan, but didn't even make it over to his laptop resting on a car hood. "This isn't it, Mr. McNeil."

"How do you know?"

"I worked on the countermeasure long enough to know this isn't it. She's trying to pass off a fake."

McNeil pulled out a gun and pointed it right at Sawyer. "I sure hope you have something more than that to offer us, Megan. Or a broken bone isn't going to be the worst of Agent Branson's problems today."

"Wait, wait! I have the real one. It's in the car."

She heard Sawyer's curse from his hunched-over form. But Sawyer was already hurt enough; she couldn't let him be shot if there was any way she could stop it. Megan backed up toward the car, her arm still protectively around Sawyer as if she could ward off the gun McNeil was pointing at him.

Megan opened the door of her car and reached under the seat to get the countermeasure. She then held it out to Jonathan. "Here. You know this is it, but you can test it anyway."

"See, now, that wasn't so difficult, was it?" McNeil asked. He put his gun back into his holster and gave his attention to Jonathan.

Megan noticed Sawyer was now standing right in front of her and was pushing her back toward the car, since the door was open.

"Get in and stay down," Sawyer whispered to her.

"What?" Megan said to him just as softly. Had she heard him right? How was Sawyer even capable of talking at all?

"Just do it, baby. Now!"

Megan dived into the car and Sawyer shut the door. She watched as Sawyer straightened and pulled a gun from the waistband of his jeans. None of McNeil's men were expecting such an abrupt, strong move from the man who had been barely conscious just a few moments before.

Especially not McNeil. Sawyer was able to get a shot off at McNeil first, who died with a surprised look on his face without even getting his gun back out.

Sawyer emptied the entire clip of his weapon, trying

to clear out anybody who might fire in their direction. He got help from somewhere up in the mountains of junk. Megan couldn't see them, but Evan and his men were covering Sawyer.

It didn't take long. In less than a minute all of McNeil's men were either dead or wounded. Nobody had suspected Sawyer capable of the move he had made.

Heck, Megan had been standing right next to him and hadn't expected him to be capable of that. She opened the car door and scrambled out and over to Sawyer. She wanted to put her arms around him, but there didn't seem to be anywhere on his body that wasn't injured.

"Sawyer, oh my gosh, are you okay? I thought you were nearly dead."

Sawyer crumpled down onto his knees. Megan looked down at his shoulder and realized blood was pouring from a wound.

Sawyer had been shot.

Megan grabbed Sawyer in her arms and helped him lie down on the ground, putting pressure on the wound to stop the bleeding. Sawyer was unconscious and losing blood fast.

Evan and his men came down from their vantage points at the top of the junk heaps. They checked the status of the DS-13 men. Most of them were dead; they secured any who weren't. Jonathan Bushman, who had hidden by a car when the bullets started flying, was led away in handcuffs by one of Evan's men, an unbelieving look on his face. Megan barely spared him a glance. He deserved whatever he had coming to him.

"Evan, we need an ambulance here. Right now!" Megan held Sawyer's head in one hand and kept pressure on the bleeding wound with the other. Sawyer wasn't stirring at all now and his color was a sickly gray.

An ambulance, this far out of town, would be too late.

Evan scrambled over to them, looking at the damage to Sawyer's body. "Damn it," Evan muttered. "Sawyer, you stay with us," he yelled down at Sawyer's unconscious form.

"An ambulance is not going to get here in time, Evan." Tears rolled down Megan's cheeks.

"We don't have to wait for an ambulance. We have something better coming—thanks to Juliet. Listen, there it is."

At first Megan couldn't hear anything over the panic roaring in her own ears. But then she did: a helicopter.

Megan's terror subsided just the tiniest bit. "Hang in there, sweetheart," she whispered in Sawyer's ear. "I've still got a lot more yelling to do before you go."

Chapter Twenty-Four

It was a tough climb out of the hospital for Sawyer. Even with the helicopter transferring him to the trauma center as fast as possible, he was in critical condition for days. It was not just because of the bullet wound, but the internal injuries and bleeding he'd suffered at the hands of McNeil's men.

Much of the early hospital stay was a blur for Sawyer. He could remember his family being there—his brothers and sister, even his parents. But all he had wanted was Megan. Once he knew she was there with him, he had felt as if he could rest. She was safe, she was next to him, it would all be okay.

When Sawyer had become more coherent, Evan had assured him that *both* copies of Ghost Shell and the countermeasure were safely in Omega's keeping. All of McNeil's men were either arrested, including Jonathan Bushman, or dead. They'd taken another huge chunk out of DS-13 and didn't expect to be having to deal with that crime syndicate group again anytime soon.

Sawyer was glad, but he was more concerned about the situation with Megan. Every time he had awakened those first few days, she had been right beside him. Sometimes holding his hand, sometimes asleep on the chair, but always there.

Surely that meant that she cared, right? That she had forgiven him for his ridiculous words? That she was willing to give their relationship a try?

Because one thing was absolutely clear to Sawyer after what had happened at the junkyard: he could not live without Megan. That tiny little scientist with her giant brain had lodged herself permanently in his heart.

All he needed was a chance to do the same to her heart. Turnabout was fair play.

But the past couple of days in the hospital, Megan hadn't been around. Sawyer had been up, walking, recovering nicely, surrounded by all his loved ones offering their support and encouragement.

All his loved ones except the most important one.

By the end of the third day without Megan, Sawyer was such a bear that his own family had threatened to disown him. The medical staff stayed as far from him as possible, only entering his room when it was necessary and leaving as quickly as possible.

It was Evan who finally addressed the issue.

"Dude, you're starting to make us all wish that bullet had hit you a few inches to the left."

"Where the hell is Megan, Evan?"

"You heard Juliet tell you she'd gotten a new job somewhere outside this area. So my guess is she's busy packing. Getting ready to leave."

If Sawyer could've reached Evan, he would've slugged him for his nonchalant attitude about Megan walking out of Sawyer's life. But Evan had known Sawyer too long and made sure he stayed out of arm's reach.

"Damn it, Evan, she can't leave me, go take another job, meet other people. I love her." Sawyer sounded like a crazy person, even to his own ears.

"Have you let her know that?"

"No. She hasn't been here in three days!"

"Well, I guess you better get to her, then, moron."

So here Sawyer was at Megan's house. Sawyer still wasn't at full speed, and the doctors had some concerns about the possibility of continued internal bleeding. But Sawyer had turned on all the charm, promised extended rest at home and had gotten released from the hospital.

And promptly drove to Megan's house.

Megan was in the process of cleaning up the mess that had been made by DS-13 and packing anything salvageable. To his surprise, Sawyer found his mother and Juliet helping her. When they saw him, his mom and Juliet discreetly made their way outside, giving Sawyer and Megan privacy.

"Hi."

Megan stopped packing the box she was working on at his greeting. "Are you supposed to be out of the hospital?"

"Well, you disappeared, so I got them to release me."

"I'm sorry, I wasn't trying to abandon you. You had your entire family there, and I have so much to do with the packing…" Megan gestured around the room with her arm.

Sawyer, known for keeping a cool head no matter what the circumstances, felt panic bubble up inside him. "No."

"No, what?" Megan's expression seemed genuinely puzzled.

"No, you can't take a new job wherever it is and leave me, and we never see each other again."

Megan looked a little concerned. "Sawyer, are you on medication that makes you loopy? Do you need to sit down or something? You're acting a little strange."

"No, I'm not on any damned medication like that, and I don't need to sit down!" Sawyer fought a losing battle with the panic. She was leaving him, for God's sake. How could she be so calm and collected? Didn't he mean anything to her at all?

Sawyer stormed over and grabbed her by one shoulder with his good hand. "I'm sorry, okay. I'm so sorry I said all that stupid stuff. I never thought you were the traitor, really. Don't leave me, Megan. Please. I love you."

"Sawyer—"

No, he couldn't let her continue. He had to make her give him a chance. "I know we haven't known each other that long, and that saying I love you is crazy. But it's true. I don't want you to move far away. I want us to be where we can see each other." A brilliant idea occurred to Sawyer. "We should get married."

Megan shook her head. "What? Sawyer, stop."

"It's okay. You can take the new job far away. I'll quit Omega and move with you and work at an FBI field office somewhere." The idea seemed brilliant to Sawyer. "Just as long as we can be together."

"Sawyer. Just listen to me—"

Sawyer didn't want to listen. He didn't want to hear all the reasons why Megan thought their relationship wouldn't work. How he had ruined it by not trusting her completely. So Sawyer did the only thing he could think of.

He kissed her.

He expected Megan to pull away, but she didn't. She stepped closer so their bodies were pressed together. Her lips were as hungry for the kiss as his were.

Eventually, Megan eased back from their kiss. Sawyer didn't want to let her go, but knew it had to happen.

"Sawyer—"

Sawyer put his forehead against hers. "Whatever you're about to say, I just want you to know I love you."

"Man, let the woman talk," Juliet said it from the doorway. "If you would shut up for just one minute, I think you might get your happily-ever-after." She grabbed a box and walked with his mom into the kitchen, leaving them alone.

"What the hell is she talking about?"

Megan smiled. "Well, if you'd stop acting like such a

crazy person and listen I would tell you that yes, I took a new job."

"I know. You're moving."

"I took a job at Omega, Sawyer. At the main headquarters, in the cyberterrorism department. I believe that's just a few floors from your office, if I'm not mistaken. I might be asking you to bring *me* coffee." Megan's smile was the most beautiful thing Sawyer had ever seen.

Sawyer wrapped his arm around Megan, pulling her against him, relief almost taking his breath away. She wasn't leaving him. He had all the time he needed to convince her how perfect they were for each other.

"And just so you know," Megan said, peeking up at him from where she was tucked against his chest, "I love you, too, Agent Branson."

Looked as if she didn't need to be convinced, after all. He always knew she had a giant brain.

* * * * *

Look for more books in Janie Crouch's
OMEGA SECTOR *miniseries later in 2015.*
You'll find them wherever
Harlequin Intrigue books are sold!

REQUEST YOUR FREE BOOKS!
2 FREE NOVELS PLUS 2 FREE GIFTS!

♦ HARLEQUIN®

INTRIGUE®

BREATHTAKING ROMANTIC SUSPENSE

YES! Please send me 2 FREE Harlequin Intrigue® novels and my 2 FREE gifts (gifts are worth about $10). After receiving them, if I don't wish to receive any more books, I can return the shipping statement marked "cancel." If I don't cancel, I will receive 6 brand-new novels every month and be billed just $4.74 per book in the U.S. or $5.24 per book in Canada. That's a savings of at least 14% off the cover price! It's quite a bargain! Shipping and handling is just 50¢ per book in the U.S. and 75¢ per book in Canada.* I understand that accepting the 2 free books and gifts places me under no obligation to buy anything. I can always return a shipment and cancel at any time. Even if I never buy another book, the two free books and gifts are mine to keep forever.

182/382 HDN F42N

Name	(PLEASE PRINT)	
Address		Apt. #
City	State/Prov.	Zip/Postal Code

Signature (if under 18, a parent or guardian must sign)

Mail to the **Harlequin® Reader Service:**
IN U.S.A.: P.O. Box 1867, Buffalo, NY 14240-1867
IN CANADA: P.O. Box 609, Fort Erie, Ontario L2A 5X3

**Are you a subscriber to Harlequin Intrigue books
and want to receive the larger-print edition?
Call 1-800-873-8635 or visit www.ReaderService.com.**

* Terms and prices subject to change without notice. Prices do not include applicable taxes. Sales tax applicable in N.Y. Canadian residents will be charged applicable taxes. Offer not valid in Quebec. This offer is limited to one order per household. Not valid for current subscribers to Harlequin Intrigue books. All orders subject to credit approval. Credit or debit balances in a customer's account(s) may be offset by any other outstanding balance owed by or to the customer. Please allow 4 to 6 weeks for delivery. Offer available while quantities last.

Your Privacy—The Harlequin® Reader Service is committed to protecting your privacy. Our Privacy Policy is available online at www.ReaderService.com or upon request from the Harlequin Reader Service.

We make a portion of our mailing list available to reputable third parties that offer products we believe may interest you. If you prefer that we not exchange your name with third parties, or if you wish to clarify or modify your communication preferences, please visit us at www.ReaderService.com/consumerchoice or write to us at Harlequin Reader Service Preference Service, P.O. Box 9062, Buffalo, NY 14269. Include your complete name and address.

HI13R

*A Texas deputy steps in to protect a vulnerable witness,
even though she could send his own father to jail…*

"You know that I'm staying here with you tonight, right,"
Colt said when he pulled to a stop in front of her house.

Elise was certain that wasn't a question, and she wanted
to insist his babysitting her wasn't necessary.

But she was afraid that it was.

Because someone wanted her dead. Had even sent
someone to end her life. And that someone had nearly
succeeded.

She'd hoped the bone-deep exhaustion would tamp
down the fear. It didn't. She was feeling both fear and
fatigue, and that wasn't a good mix.

Nor was having Colt around.

However, the alternative was her being alone in her
house that was miles from town or her nearest neighbor.
And for just the rest of the night, she wasn't ready for
the alone part. In the morning though, she would have to
do something to remedy it. Something that didn't include
Colt and her under the same roof.

For now though, that was exactly what was about to
happen.

They got out of his truck, the sleet still spitting at them,
and the air so bitterly cold that it burned her lungs with
each breath she took. Elise's hands were still shaking,
and when she tried to unlock the front door of her house,
she dropped the gob of keys, the metal sound clattering

onto the weathered wood porch. Colt reached for them at the same time she did, and their heads ended up colliding.

Right on her stitches.

The pain shot through her, and even though Elise tried to choke back the groan, she didn't quite succeed.

"Sorry." Colt cursed and snatched the keys from her to unlock the door. He definitely wasn't shaking.

"Wait here," he ordered the moment they stepped into the living room. He shut the door, gave her a stay-put warning glance and drew his gun before he started looking around.

Only then did Elise realize that someone—another hit man maybe—could be already hiding inside. Waiting to kill her.

Sweet heaven.

When was this going to end?

As the threats to Elise Nichols escalate, so does the tension between her and sexy cowboy Colt McKinnon!

Don't miss their heart-stopping story when
THE DEPUTY'S REDEMPTION,
part of USA TODAY *bestselling author*
Delores Fossen's **SWEETWATER RANCH** *miniseries,*
goes on sale in March 2015.